Amish ᴦalse Witness

Ettie Smith Amish Mysteries

Book 8

Samantha Price

Chapter 1

"I have a secret I should've shared with someone long ago, but didn't."

Ettie stared at Florence, an older sister she hadn't seen for a long time, as Florence stood on the doorstep of the house Ettie shared with their eldest sister, Elsa-May. The years had whitened Florence's hair or at least the part of her hair that was seen in front of her prayer *kapp*. She'd always parted her hair in the middle and pulled it back tightly, wearing her *kapp* very much to the front of her head.

"Come in."

As Florence stepped into the house, Ettie yelled out for Elsa-May, who came out of the kitchen wiping her hands on a hand towel.

"Florence!" Elsa-May embraced her younger sister.

"It's nice to see you both after so long. When was the last time?"

"You were here for Jeremiah's wedding."

"That's right, I was."

Elsa-May glanced down at the bag in her sister's hand and asked the question Ettie had been too afraid to ask. "Have you come to stay?"

"I've come to tell you something."

"Let's sit down in the living room," Ettie said with a light touch on Florence's elbow.

Elsa-May's small white fluffy dog bounded toward Florence.

"You've got a dog?"

"Jah, this is Snowy. I'm certain I mentioned him in my letters."

"You might have." Florence looked at Ettie. "What happened to Ginger?"

"He died years ago, Florence." Her comments proved to Ettie that she never bothered reading any of their letters.

"I can't remember everything. I'm sorry to hear about that. I know you had him for a very long time."

"I did indeed."

"Ettie got me Snowy."

2

"It wasn't me, Elsa-May." She turned to Florence. "It was our neighbor who brought him over and then Elsa-May fell in love with him. The dog, not our neighbor."

Florence giggled.

Elsa-May explained, "Our neighbor knew someone who worked at the dog shelter and that's how we ended up with Snowy."

"I'm sure that's all very interesting, but right now could someone make me a cup of *kaffe?*"

"Who did you stay with when you came to Jeremiah's wedding?" Elsa-May asked.

"I stayed with a lovely lady called Rebecca. She owns a bakery in town and lives not far from it."

"That's Ruth," Ettie said.

"*Jah,* that's right. She's a lovely woman and she had a bed for me."

Ettie didn't say anything else. There was no point; she was always on the losing end with all of her sisters. It wasn't easy being the youngest.

"I would like to stay with the two of you. Is there anything wrong with that?"

3

"Not at all. It's lovely to have you stay with us. It's just that our house is so small and we don't want to make you uncomfortable," Elsa-May explained.

"Well, I'm fine with it, so let's not have any more talk about it."

"I'll get you that tea, Florence," Ettie said.

"Nee. It was *kaffe."*

Minutes later, they were gathered around the kitchen table.

"Do you remember when I left the community for a time before I was married?" Florence asked them.

"When you were off gallivanting with that country singer?" Elsa-May asked.

"Country and Western," Florence corrected her. "I think they call it that now, I can't remember what they called it back in the fifties."

"Then you left him and came back to us," Ettie added.

She shook her head. "I didn't leave him. He was arrested for murder and I came back to the community."

"You were forced to leave him?" Ettie asked trying to recall the blurry details from years ago.

"*Jah.* Now his grandson has been arrested for a murder he didn't commit."

"His grandson? Is there something you're not telling us? Where would he have had time to have a child if he was in prison, unless...? Did you have a child with him?"

"Of course not! Always the oldest aren't you, Elsa-May—thinking you have to watch over everyone—thinking the worst? Tsk, tsk." Florence shook her head.

"*Nee!*" Elsa-May said as she leaned back in her chair.

"Tell us about the grandson. What's his name?"

"His name's Dustin Gandara. I read in the newspaper that he was arrested and I knew he was Morrie's grandson. He's only twenty. They pulled him over and said he was driving under the influence, and then they forced him to take a DNA test."

"Forced him? Can they do that?"

5

"Nee, I don't think they can, but he probably agreed. Anyway, the DNA is a match to a girl who was murdered six weeks ago on the campus of his college."

"I don't understand what you're saying. How can his DNA be a match to a girl?"

"They found his DNA under the girl's fingernails."

"I see, that makes more sense," Elsa-May said.

"And you don't think he did it?" Ettie asked.

"Nee, I visited him and he said he didn't do it. He wasn't drinking or even speeding and the police pulled him over. What disturbs me is why they pulled him over in the first place. How did they know his DNA was going to be a match?"

"Maybe they didn't," Elsa-May said.

"He was set up. That's what he said."

"By the police?" Ettie asked.

"By someone who contacted them—obviously," Florence said.

"What does this have to do with the secret you were going on about just now?

"Morrie gave me a gun. Don't you see?"

"Nee!" Ettie and Elsa-May chorused.

"The gun was found in Dustin's car and now they're saying the gun was used in two murders in the last two years. But it couldn't have been because I had it hidden in my house—up until it burned down around six weeks ago."

"That's dreadful!" Ettie said.

"How do you know it's the same gun?" Elsa-May asked.

Ettie narrowed her eyes at her oldest sister. "Elsa-May, Florence just said that her house burned down."

"I heard, but she's here in front of us, so I know she escaped unharmed. She was telling us about the gun. I'm intrigued to know more."

Florence continued, "Dustin saw it when the police pulled him over and searched the car. They asked him if it was his and he told them he'd never seen it before. He described the gun to me and said it had the letters MW painted in bright yellow and the trigger was painted blue. The gun hadn't been

7

there, in the car, until then. Dustin told me either the police planted it there or someone put it there just before he was pulled over."

"The woman was shot? The woman who was found on campus—she was shot with this gun?"

"Nee, she was strangled, but his DNA was found under her fingernails. He was set up. They burned down my house so I wouldn't notice the gun was missing. Then they planted the gun in Dustin's car and got him pulled over on a false accusation that he was speeding."

"I thought you said it was for driving under the influence."

"That's right, Ettie, it was. Don't you see?"

"Nee, we don't see anything. It's all confusing. How do you know that the boy's not guilty?"

"He's a man now and he's not guilty because they admitted he wasn't driving under the influence, but by that time they had the gun and his DNA. If he was guilty, he wouldn't have said yes to the DNA test."

Ettie and Elsa-May looked at each other.

"They tricked him, can't you see that?" Florence asked.

"They might have tricked him, but you can't escape the fact that his DNA was found under the girl's fingernails. They don't get things like that wrong."

"What about the gun that was taken out of my *haus?* Then they burned the place down to cover their tracks. It was just the next day that Dustin was arrested. I'm telling you, things aren't adding up. Don't you want to know who shot those other two people? It wasn't Dustin, and the people weren't shot with Willis Gandara's gun. They couldn't have been, because it was in my house."

"Who's Willis Gandara?"

"Morrie—his manager changed his name to Wylie Morris before he became famous. His real name is Willis Gandara. I only knew him as Wylie Morris and everyone around him called him Morrie, so I've always called him Morrie."

"That makes sense," Ettie agreed.

"I've come here so you can help me to help Dustin."

"What's happening with your *haus?*" Elsa-May asked.

"Linda and Theodore are arranging for it to be rebuilt. The fire started while I was at the Sunday meeting. They knew I would be out. They had it all arranged."

"Who are 'they'?"

Florence opened her eyes widely. "Whoever stole the gun."

Ettie tugged at the strings of her *kapp* hoping she'd be able to help her sister, but first, they'd have to figure out if Dustin was innocent.

"Mary Schwartz told me that the two of you help the police sometimes. I thought you might be able to speak with them and find out what's really going on."

"We know a detective who sometimes asks for our help when there's any community involvement in a crime."

"And your friend, Dustin, isn't in the community.

That could make him reluctant to help us or give us any information," Elsa-May added.

"Surely he could help. They burned down my house so they could steal my gun. Wouldn't the police want to know that?"

Elsa-May looked at Ettie, and asked, "What do you think? We could ask Detective Kelly a few questions."

"I suppose we could."

"Oh goodie! Can I come along?" Florence asked.

"*Jah,* you'll have to, but you must let us do most of the talking. He's a bit gruff sometimes," Elsa-May explained.

Ettie's eyes drifted to Florence's suitcase. "Where do you plan on staying while you're here?"

"Why here, of course."

Ettie nibbled on a fingernail. "We only have two bedrooms."

"Then I'll take the couch."

Elsa-May said, "We could arrange for you to stay with Jeremiah and Ava, they've got plenty of room at their place."

"Nee! I won't stay with someone I don't know. I'll stay on the couch here."

"You know Jeremiah, my grandson. You came to his wedding not that long ago."

Florence moved from one of the chairs to the couch. "This is nice and comfy." She stared at the chairs in front of her. "Are they from the old *haus?"*

"Jah, they're *Mamm* and *Dat's* old chairs," Ettie said.

Florence laughed. "They should've been tossed out years ago."

"We like them," Elsa-May said.

"Well, you like them, Elsa-May. I kept saying to get rid of them. They're not very sturdy."

"They are now, since Jeremiah fixed them."

"Jah, but for how long?" Ettie said.

"I think they were *grossdaddi's* chairs. Antiques are fine and good, but not so much when they're chairs because they can collapse under people. Anyway, it's settled, I'll sleep on the couch unless one of you is prepared to give up your bed for a guest?" Florence looked from one sister to the other.

"I've got a bad back," Elsa-May said.

"Have you?" Ettie asked, wondering why she'd never heard of it.

"It plays up sometimes. I'm not one to complain about things," Elsa-May added with a twitch of her lips.

Florence turned her attention to Ettie. "How about you, Ettie? The older sister should have preference."

"And I'm the eldest," Elsa-May was quick to add.

"That rule shouldn't apply in my own home. You see, no one ever stays at our place. If someone comes to visit us, we always find a friend close by that they can stay with."

"There was that time Jeremiah stayed here, Ettie. Didn't he sleep in your bed and you slept on the couch?" Elsa-May said.

Ettie's jaw dropped open. "That was an extreme situation. That was when we had that   kidnapper prowling around trying to take the *boppli.*"

Florence frowned. "What *boppli?*"

"Someone left him here at our door…"

"It's a long story," Elsa-May said cutting Ettie off. "We'll tell you about it another time."

"You two lead exciting lives by the sounds of it. So, Ettie, you gave up your bed for Elsa-May's grandson?"

"Jah, but it was only one time and we…"

"Then, it's settled. You can sleep on the couch and since I'm a guest, I'll sleep in your bed."

Ettie's mouth turned down at the corners. If she insisted on sleeping in her own bed, she'd feel mean and she wasn't a mean person. "I think you'd be more comfortable staying at Jeremiah's *haus.*"

"He and his wife are newlyweds." Florence shook her head. "I wouldn't feel comfortable. I'd be under their feet."

"And I wouldn't feel comfortable sleeping on the couch," Ettie blurted out.

Florence stared at Ettie. "If I'm not wanted here, I'll have to go back home. That's right, I forgot—I

14

don't have a home."

Elsa-May chuckled.

Florence didn't stop there. "I thought you'd want to help an innocent person sitting in a jail cell for something he didn't do."

"We *are* helping you." Ettie sighed. "Okay, okay. I'll sleep on the couch."

"Why don't you both take it in turns? One night Ettie sleeps on the couch and one night you sleep on the couch, Florence. I'd take a turn too, but then there's my back." Elsa-May leaned forward slightly to put her hand on her back.

Florence sighed. "Okay. We'll take turns. Agreed, Ettie? Will that stop your brattish whining?"

Ettie nodded, not reacting to Florence's sniping and not happy about having another older sister in the house to boss her about. One was bad enough.

Chapter 2

Ettie approached the officer behind the front desk at the police station. "We're here to see Detective Kelly. Is he here right now?"

The officer took a moment to draw his eyes away from the computer in front of him. He looked at Ettie and then looked at each of her two sisters. "All three of you?"

"Yes, that's right. All of us to see Detective Kelly."

"Isn't there usually only two of you?"

"Yes, that's right." Ettie smiled taking a small amount of delight in the officer's confusion.

"I'll see if he's free."

"So he's here?" Elsa-May asked.

"I believe he is," he said as he picked up the phone's receiver.

When he spoke to Detective Kelly, Ettie turned around and smiled at her sister, Florence.

Florence leaned in to Ettie. "What do we do now?"

"He'll see if Detective Kelly is in and then we'll have to wait for him to come out."

Florence scowled. "How long will we have to wait?"

"Not long. Sometimes we've had to wait more than an hour when he's been busy."

Florence shook her head. "I don't like waiting."

"Sometimes we just have to," Elsa-May whispered.

Florence pouted. "Well, I think it's rude to keep us waiting."

Elsa-May said, "But he didn't know we were coming. We don't have an appointment."

"It's not a very efficient service."

Elsa-May and Ettie glanced at each other with raised eyebrows.

The officer hung up the phone, and said, "He'll be five minutes. Take a seat." He kept staring at them until Ettie pulled Florence by her sleeve, showing her where to sit.

The three elderly Amish ladies sat in a row in the waiting area.

Five minutes later, Detective Kelly appeared at the end of the hallway where he had a clear view of them. He stopped in his tracks as though stunned and then proceeded towards them, stopping in front of them.

Ettie pushed herself carefully to her feet. "Detective Kelly, we'd like you to meet our sister, Florence Lapp."

His eyes widened as he stared at Florence. "There are three of you?"

"Oh no, we have many more sisters."

"And some brothers," Elsa-May added.

"Can we take a moment of your time?" Ettie asked.

He reached out his hand. "Nice to meet you, Mrs. Lapp. I'm Detective Kelly."

"Nice to make your acquaintance," Florence said, shaking his hand firmly.

"Do you have a moment?" Elsa-May asked, repeating Ettie's query as she stood up.

"Of course, this way please." Kelly led the way back to his office. He pulled out an extra chair for Florence to sit on. Normally there were only two chairs in front of his desk. He took up a pen and notepad. "How can I help you, ladies?"

Florence spoke first. "We're here to help you."

"With what?"

"With an investigation that your police friends have got wrong."

Ettie frowned, knowing this was not the way to persuade Kelly to help them. Tact had never been a strong trait in her family.

Kelly leaned forward and clasped his hands on the desk not taking his eyes from Florence. "I'm listening."

"It all started back in the fifties…"

Kelly breathed out heavily and leaned back in his chair. "The fifties? Not the roaring twenties or the thrifty thirties?"

"I was born in the twenties, though, so maybe you could say that's when it started."

"I have no idea why you're here, Mrs. Lapp, but

can't we bypass the fifties and skip to the present day—please?" He glanced at his watch.

Florence shook her head. "I need to tell you first about the gun that Morrie gave me and that was in the fifties. If I don't tell you that, nothing else will make sense."

Kelly's eyes glazed over. "Okay, continue."

"Back in the fifties, I met Morrie and I was swept off my feet. I left the community and went on tour with Wylie Morris."

Detective Kelly leaned forward, suddenly keenly interested. "You knew Wylie Morris?"

"I was his girlfriend."

"You were?"

Florence nodded.

Kelly's face lit up. "That brings back memories. I remember my mother playing his records. They were LPs back then. She was a fan, a big fan. Whatever became of him?"

"He went to jail for murder."

He nodded. "Yes. I remember reading something about that now. So all his money couldn't save him from jail?"

Elsa-May leaned forward, "Are you implying that money can get someone off a charge, Detective?"

"Not at all. I wasn't implying anything of the sort. I was just pointing out that the rich and the poor are judged the same in our legal system—as it should be."

Ettie added, "Phooey! They aren't treated equal at all. How is it fair that the rich can afford better lawyers, and there are many people in jail waiting for trials simply because they can't afford bail? How's that fair when the rich people get out and the poor don't?"

Kelly scratched his face. "You're right, Mrs. Smith, none of that is fair about the bail system—and there are many other things in life that aren't fair—but if we're going to debate about things like that we could be here until next week. While you might have the time, I don't."

Ettie pushed her lips together, not happy about him thinking she didn't have anything better to do with her time just because she was old. Would he have said that to a younger person?

"Now getting back to Wylie Morris, Mrs. Lapp. You mentioned a gun?"

Elsa-Mayhiccuppedloudly. Sheputherfingertips to her lips and gave a little giggle. "Excuse me."

Detective Kelly glared at her before he looked back at Florence. "I'm listening," he said.

"He gave me a gun—Wylie did. It was only for protection because he was worried about me."

"He said that's why he gave it to you?"

"That is not exactly the point of my story. You see, the gun that Wylie gave me was taken from my house and planted in Morrie's grandson's car, and now he's been accused of murder."

Elsa-May leaned forward and hiccupped again. "Whoops!"

Florence glanced at Elsa-May.

Ettie explained further, "The police said that the gun was used in two murders in the last two years."

"And it couldn't have been because it had been in my house and never left," Florence added.

Florence told the detective the whole story.

The detective asked more questions surrounding Dustin's arrest, the drunk-driving charge, the murder charge, and finding the gun in his car.

"It's all very intriguing, I must say."

"So you'll help us?" Ettie asked.

The detective frowned. "Help you to do what?"

"Justin's innocent. We need you to prove it," Ettie said.

Florence put her hand on Ettie's. "His name is Dustin, not Justin."

Elsa-May hiccupped again.

Ettie continued, "Oh, sorry. As I was saying, Dustin's innocent."

"Why would you think he's innocent? Didn't you say they found his DNA under a dead girl's fingernails?" He looked at each of the three women in turn. "It sounds like he's guilty to me, straight up, but I suppose there's always the chance that the DNA might have been under her fingernails for some other reason. It doesn't mean that he killed her—necessarily. That's what his lawyer would argue at any rate."

Elsa-May hiccupped again.

"Mrs. Lutz, would you like some water?"

"Yes, please. I don't know what brought this on."

Kelly pressed his intercom button and asked for a bottle of water.

Florence opened her mouth to speak and Kelly lifted up his hand. "Let's just get your sister settled first."

A young officer brought a bottle of water in and handed it to Kelly.

"I hope you don't think I can drink out of a bottle. Can I have a glass?" Elsa-May asked.

"Get a glass will you?" Kelly asked the officer.

The young officer returned with a glass.

Kelly opened the bottle, poured some water into the glass and pushed it across the desk to Elsa-May.

"Thank you." Elsa-May took a couple of mouthfuls.

Florence said, "Are you all good now, Elsa-May?"

Elsa-May nodded. "I hope so."

Florence looked back at Detective Kelly.

"Someone came into my home and took something that didn't belong to them, and then they burned down my home."

"That's something I can look into. What's your address, Mrs. Lapp?"

Florence rattled off her address and Kelly wrote it down.

"I'll find out what I can." He looked up at the three elderly women. "Anything else?"

"Will you look into his arrest, too?"

He tilted his computer monitor toward him. "Name?"

"Dustin Gandara."

"Date of birth?"

"I'm not certain."

Kelly tapped a couple of buttons. "Here it is." He read what was on his screen. "I'll look into the report on his arrest, and I'll have a chat with the arresting officers. It conveniently falls within my jurisdiction."

"Okay, good. Thank you, Detective," Florence said.

"I'll find out about the gun and those murders."

"Would you?" Ettie asked.

He nodded. "You've been helpful to me over the years, Mrs. Smith, it's the least I can do."

Florence patted Ettie on her shoulder and Ettie turned and smiled at her.

"Where can I reach you, Mrs. Lapp?"

"I'm staying with Ettie and Elsa-May until my house is rebuilt."

"That long?" Ettie blurted out before she could stop herself. She squirmed in her seat at the thought of every second night on the couch for many months. They'd also have another person in their small home, which was really only big enough for two people and one small dog.

Florence stared at Ettie. "Yes, that long. Now come along. You heard the man; he's busy and we shouldn't hold him up. He's got crooks to catch."

"Thank you, Mrs. Lapp. Why don't you come by tomorrow afternoon and I'll tell you what I've learned."

"You can work that fast?" Florence asked.

"I can." Detective Kelly's face beamed.

"We can come back, can't we?" Florence directed the question at Elsa-May.

"How about you come to our house tomorrow afternoon, Detective, and we'll be sure to have a nice pot of coffee ready for you?"

"And cake!" Ettie added.

He smiled. "I'd be delighted. I can't pass up an offer like that. I'll be there between four and five unless something unexpected turns up."

Elsa-May hiccupped loudly again before they walked out of his office.

Ettie thought she heard a loud sigh just as she closed the door behind them.

Chapter 3

The next afternoon Detective Kelly sat in Elsa-May and Ettie's living room with the three sisters.

"Mrs. Lapp. I made some inquiries…"

"You don't have to keep calling me Mrs. Lapp; it's so formal."

"Florrie, I made some inquiries."

"My name's not Florrie. I don't like to be called that."

The detective laughed. "I'm sorry, I had an Aunt Florrie once."

"What does that have to do with me?"

The detective stared at Florence for a moment while his mouth attempted to form words. "I always assumed that Florrie was short for Florence."

"Well, was it in your aunt's case?"

Detective Kelly rubbed the side of his face. "I'm not certain now, come to think of it."

"And do you normally make such assumptions

in your line of work, Detective? I thought people in your profession dealt in facts," Florence said.

"I don't make those assumptions when it involves work. Not when it's about a case." He shook his head. "Can we start again?"

"Please do," Florence said.

"Now I can see the family resemblance. I made some inquiries, *Florence*."

When he emphasized her name, she smiled. "And what did you find out?"

"The incident report from your house states that the fire was started in the bedroom—most likely from a candle that was left burning on the nightstand. Nothing in the report suggests arson. There was absolutely no evidence of the use of accelerants."

"Maybe there was."

Kelly shook his head. "They're very thorough. There were no signs of any accelerants. They classed it as an accidental fire due to the candle in the bedroom burning down, or tipping over."

"It's never tipped over before."

"Do you have a cat who could've knocked it over?"

"No, I've never had a cat. Someone came into my house to start the fire. All they had to do was tip the candle over."

"That's probably how they started the fire. Normally, deliberately lit fires use accelerants."

"I always keep a lit candle in my bedroom throughout the night. I find it calming."

"Did you forget to blow it out that morning?"

"I never blow it out in the morning. I just leave it to burn."

"Well, that's what started the fire. According to statistics, the most common place for home fires to start is in a bedroom."

"There were no drafts or breezes. All the windows and all the doors were closed. I always make certain of that. I like to burn the candles down because I don't like to blow them out—it's bad luck."

Detective Kelly's eyes opened wide. "No! I didn't know that." He looked at Elsa-May and

Ettie.

"Our sister doesn't necessarily hold all of our beliefs," Elsa-May explained.

"She's slightly alternative," Ettie said.

"Well, I'll take that as a compliment. I don't want to be the same as everybody else. Do you see my point detective?" Florence asked.

"I suppose so."

"Ever since I've lived in that house, I've always let the candle burn down in the morning. It's a slow burning candle that lasts all night and through to the morning. It was probably due to burn itself down and go out by around midday or just before. I'm convinced the fire was deliberate."

"Well, that's not what the investigators think."

"They can think what they want."

"Was your house under insurance, Mrs. Lapp?" Kelly asked.

"That's just wasting money. I don't believe in insurance. My son-in-law and his friend are rebuilding the house for me. What do I need insurance for?"

"When was the last time you saw the gun?"

"I had the gun under my bed. I checked it every night before I went to sleep."

"Why? Were you expecting someone to break in?"

"Morrie gave it to me for protection. It would be rude if I had ignored the purpose he gave me the gun for."

"That Sunday morning of the fire, you left for your meeting—was the gun under your bed that morning?"

"I'm saying, I saw it there the night before, like every other night. I didn't check on the gun in the morning. That wasn't my habit. And there was no report of the gun when they sifted through the remains of the house. Someone must've taken it."

"I see."

"Do you? Someone burned down the house thinking I'd forget about the gun. They wanted to get it."

Ettie interrupted, "Detective, did you find out about the murders connected with the gun they found in Dustin's car?"

"Good question, Mrs. Smith. The gun was used in two armed hold-ups in the past two years."

"That's what I was told when I went to visit Dustin in prison."

"What you might not know is that the first one was a supermarket holdup and the next one was at a gas station."

"Why didn't the people just hand over the money? That way they wouldn't have been killed."

"That's another good point. I'll have a talk with the officers; tomorrow I'll be able to tell you more."

"Ettie, I think you don't believe the gun is the same one I had under my bed, but it is," Florence insisted.

Ettie frowned at her sister's comment because she had no such opinion about the gun.

Before she could answer, Kelly asked, "Mrs. Lapp, who knew you had the gun?"

"I can't say exactly. I don't know who knew about it."

"Have a good think about it because   it's vital

that you remember." He opened the file he brought with him and pulled out a photo of a gun. "Is this the gun you say is yours?"

"That's it! That's my gun. I looked at it every night over the past few years—ever since my children moved out of the house leaving me all alone. My husband died fifteen years ago." She took her eyes off the photo of the gun to stare at the detective. "This is the gun Morrie gave me."

"Detective, was there any connection between the two people killed by the gun? The two people in the holdups?" Elsa-May asked.

"I'll look into it. It seems unlikely—they were just in the wrong place at the wrong time, but as I said, I'll know more when I get those reports tomorrow."

"Thank you, Detective," Ettie said.

"I'll let you know the dates that those people were killed and then I want you to think back and try to remember who visited your house. If that is indeed the gun, then someone must've used it at least twice and put it back."

Florence nodded. "Yes, I have a good memory. Once I have the dates, I'll work out who was in my house. And then we'll have the killer."

"Well, I hope so, but if not, at least it might give us a bit more information," Kelly said.

"So you agree that it's the same gun?" Elsa-May inquired of the detective.

"I can't say for certain." Kelly rubbed his nose. "We'll see if we can get some information on any guns that Wylie Morris might have purchased."

"Anything else?" Ettie asked.

A smile tugged at the corners of Kelly's mouth. "I was promised cake."

The ladies laughed.

Elsa-May stood. "I'll get the cake and the coffee."

"Do you want help?" Florence asked.

"No, you keep talking with Detective Kelly."

"What did you learn about Dustin's arrest?" Ettie asked the detective while Elsa-May disappeared into the kitchen.

"Nothing out of the ordinary. He was swerving

36

across the road and that's why he was pulled over. Because they didn't have a mobile breath tester, they invited him to come down to the station and he agreed. While he was waiting at the station, they asked if he'd volunteer a DNA sample, and he agreed to that as well."

"Isn't that unusual? To ask for a DNA sample of someone who's been suspected of drunk driving? What does that have to do with DNA?"

"It sounds a little unusual, but by then they'd searched his car and found the gun, you see."

"They searched his car for a drunk-driving charge?" Ettie asked.

"It seems a little odd that they searched his car. Isn't that illegal to do that without permission?" Florence asked.

"Not if they're suspicious that there might've been drugs or something illegal in the car. Suspicion of illegal activity or of something connected with a crime makes the search legal."

"Is that what they're saying?"

Detective Kelly nodded. "Another thing that   I

think you don't know, Florence, is that Dustin had graze marks on his face when he was pulled over. They looked to be scratches. I saw the photos. He claims he didn't know how they got there. They were faint but they were there."

Florence's jaw dropped.

"That's not good," Elsa-May said.

"Does Dustin have a lawyer, Florence?" Ettie asked.

"I believe one has been appointed to defend him."

"A good one?"

Detective Kelly said, "You know his lawyer, Ettie. You met him a year or two ago."

"The only lawyer I'm familiar with is the young man in the baseball cap."

Kelly smiled. "Yes, that's the one. I can't recall his name off the top of my head, but I recognized his name when I saw it. He seems to be a very efficient fellow."

Elsa-May brought out the tray of tea and coffee and cake, with Snowy following her.

Detective Kelly bounded to his feet. "I'll help you with that, Elsa-May." He took the tray out of her hands and placed it down on the low table in between the couch and the chairs.

Chapter 4

After Detective Kelly had swallowed a few mouthfuls of coffee and eaten half a piece of cake, he sorted through papers in the file he'd brought with him. "I've written out a list of what I want you ladies to do."

"Just let us know," Ettie said.

Kelly continued, "Florence, I want you to come into the station at midday tomorrow and I'll give you the dates your gun was used in those two murders. Then you can try to jog your memory as to who visited you on those dates. If the gun is yours, the person would've needed to use the gun and get it back to you before you noticed it missing."

"Yes, before nightfall. I'll do that." Florence nodded.

"What would you like us to do?" Ettie asked.

"I'll try to find out if there was any connection between the two people who were killed in the robberies," Kelly said.

"Then we need to find out who else could've killed that poor young woman. Who would've wanted her dead?" Elsa-May said.

"I think that's something that you need to leave up to the professionals, Elsa-May. I'll see what the investigators have found out so far." The detective wagged his finger at Elsa-May and Ettie. "Don't you two ladies go poking around. Someone's been murdered and if we don't have the right person in custody you could find yourselves in serious danger."

"He doesn't know the girl at all," Florence said. "Dustin told me he didn't know the girl—the young woman who was killed."

"You admitted to only meeting the boy twice, so how can you trust that he's telling the truth?" Kelly asked.

"I'm a pretty good reader of people, Detective Kelly. He visited me the first time when he started college nearby. Anyway, I haven't reached my age without learning something about human nature."

She pointed to him. "Take you for example."

Kelly picked up his coffee mug and took a mouthful.

Florence continued, "You're not married, you live in an apartment where you know exactly where everything is. You're fanatically clean, and organized to a T. You have no pets; you don't like animals and have no desire to own any of any kind. You thought at one time that you'd like to be married, but you have no time to think about it. You don't look after yourself and you live on fast food."

He shook his head, grinning as he placed his cup down. "I'm cutting down on the fast food." Kelly laughed. "Either of your sisters could've given you that information, Mrs. Lapp."

"We haven't said anything to her," Elsa-May insisted.

"It's a fairly accurate estimation, Mrs. Lapp, I can tell you that, but it's far different from knowing if someone who is looking you in the eye is telling you the truth or a lie."

Florence laughed. "I have raised eight children—you don't think I've heard it all in my lifetime? I know the signs of a lie—suddenly breathing more deeply, a slight flush in the cheeks, dilated pupils, explaining something too hard or giving too many facts about the situation. There's more, but I won't go on."

"Okay, I get the picture. Just leave room for doubt, though. I don't want you to be disappointed if Dustin is found guilty."

"It doesn't make sense that he would give a DNA sample voluntarily if he'd just murdered somebody."

"Florence does have a point, Detective," Ettie said, reaching for a piece of cake.

"What I'm saying is sometimes we're surprised by people and their actions. He could've willingly provided the sample simply because that's what an innocent person would do. I know you think the grandson of your good friend isn't a murderer and I'm going along with you out of respect for your two sisters." He nodded toward Ettie and Elsa-

May.

"That's good of you, thank you," Florence said. The detective added, "But he very likely might be a murderer. I'm going to look into things because I admit I have been wrong in the past myself."

Elsa-May asked, "Do you know anything about the young woman who was murdered?"

Her question was directed to the detective, but Florence answered. "All I know is that she went to the same college as Dustin, but he never met her. Now they're saying he did it."

"Are you sure he's telling the truth?"

"Yeah, I am."

* * *

"You do realize that Detective Kelly gave us things to do simply to stop us from investigating?" Elsa-May said to Ettie.

"*Jah,* I was thinking that myself. He's trying to keep us out of trouble."

"He didn't want us finding anything out   about

the two men who were killed, or the young woman who was killed on campus."

"What shall we do?" Florence asked.

"What about that young lawyer, Ettie? Surely he can give us some information?"

"Excellent idea, Elsa-May. And we're going to have to find out more about the unfortunate young woman."

"How do we do that?" Florence asked.

"We'll have our friend, Ava, search things on the computer for us at the library."

"Jeremiah's *fraa?*"

"That's the one."

"She's found out all sorts of things for us in the past by searching things on the Internet."

Elsa-May added, "And it's useful that she's got a friend who works at the DMV."

Ettie said, "I'll call her tomorrow."

"Tomorrow? Why not right now?" Elsa-May urged.

"Okay. I'll call her now."

Florence shook her head. "That poor boy is

sitting in the jail cell for a crime he didn't do."

"He does have a very good solicitor. Elsa-May and I met him once. He was very helpful."

"Denke to you both for helping me to help Dustin."

A few moments later, Ettie hurried to the shanty that housed the telephone that the Amish on their street used.

"Ava, is that you?"

"Ettie?"

"Jah, it's me. I didn't expect you to get to the phone so soon."

"I just got home and I'm in the barn right by it."

"Gut!"

"What is it?"

"Do you remember my *schweschder* and Jeremiah's *ant,* Florence?"

"Jah. She came to our wedding."

"Well, she's here staying with us because her house burned down."

"That's terrible! When did that happen?"

"About a week or so ago, I think. She didn't

exactly say when."

"Would you like her to stay here? I know your *haus* is quite small."

"That's very kind of you, but that's not the reason I'm calling."

"What is it?"

"We need your help with something on the computer."

"You want me to look something up for you?"

"Jah, and time is of the essence." Ettie proceeded to give her all the information she had on Dustin and the murder he'd been accused of.

"Okay, I've got that written down, I'll get onto it tomorrow morning at the library."

"Can you stop by at our home afterward?"

"Of course."

"We also need all the names that are connected to Allissa Thomas including friends, family, and if you can, the attending officers at the crime scene. And it would be helpful if you could find out what friends she had in common with Dustin Gandara. Dustin claims he didn't know her at all."

"I'll do my best."

"Denke, Ava."

"Why don't you come to the library with me?"

"I could. What time will you be there?"

"I've got a few things first thing in the morning, but I'll be there by ten."

"That might work for us. I'll have to check with the others, though, so don't count on us being there."

"Okay."

Chapter 5

Ettie headed home and as she walked in the door, her two sisters faced her. "First thing tomorrow we'll pay a visit to the lawyer."

"I want you both to come to my appointment with the detective. He's going to give me the dates that my gun was used to shoot those two people in the holdups."

"Elsa-May and I will go with you, and then we'll go from there to see the lawyer. I know where his office is, but I don't know if he'll be there. If only I remembered his name, I could phone him and make an appointment."

"We'll have to hope he's there. Anyway, by that time we might have some information from Ava."

"Ava said she'd be at the library at about ten. Why don't we meet her there first, and then we'll know right away if she finds anything?"

"We might as well," Elsa-May said. "So it's the library, then the police-station and then the lawyer.

It'll be a busy day."

"*Denke* both of you for doing this. I'm glad you believe me. I want to do everything I can for Morrie's sake."

"You'd do the same for us. Now, let's get the dinner on. And you don't have to keep thanking us."

"You can thank me by giving me my bed back," Ettie said.

Florence laughed as though Ettie were joking.

When Florence made no further comment, Ettie thought it best to drop the subject. The couch wasn't that bad, but it was annoying that Florence refused to stay with Ava and Jeremiah. Ava even offered that Florence could stay at her house. The three women walked into the kitchen, and then Ettie pulled out some vegetables. They all sat and peeled the vegetables for dinner.

"Florence, what became of Morrie? You said he went to jail on a murder charge–did he ever get out?" Ettie asked.

"I've been wondering that myself. Who did he

murder?" Elsa-May asked.

"I said he didn't do it and I don't want to talk about it." Florence pushed her lips together firmly.

"You made it sound like you and he were still together when he went to jail, so when did he have a child? Was it before you and he were together? He couldn't have fathered one in jail."

"He had one boy, he was only a few years old when I took up with Morrie. Morrie was never married to the mother. She had her hand out for money all the time."

"Morrie wouldn't have been short of a dollar, would he? Detective Kelly recognized his name, so it seems he would've been well known back then."

"He spent money as fast as he made it—probably faster. He had a good lifestyle. To answer your question, Ettie, he's probably still in jail. I don't know for certain. I visited him once, but he told me not to come back. I didn't. I returned to the community, got baptized, and gave up my life of sin. Dustin told me when he turned eighteen he visited Morrie once, but after that Morrie refused all his visits."

"So Morrie and Dustin connected at some stage, even though Dustin's father and Morrie rarely saw one another?"

"When Dustin's father became an adult, he visited Morrie in prison, but I don't know what happened after that. Maybe Morrie told him to stay away too."

"Did you ever meet Dustin's father?"

"I saw him a few times when he was a boy."

"And what of the person Morrie was accused of killing?"

The potato slipped from Florence's hand and she stared at Ettie. "He didn't do it. He was framed. I said I don't want to talk about it."

Ettie was a little concerned. Wasn't it too much of a coincidence that Morrie was convicted of murder and now his grandson was on a murder charge—could they both be innocent? Ettie felt Elsa-May staring at her and when she looked at her, Elsa-May raised her eyebrows and Ettie knew she had the same concerns.

"Neither of you believes me now, do you? That's why I'm keeping quiet about who they say Morrie killed."

Elsa-May handed Florence the potato that had skidded across the table.

"Do you want to talk about it now?" Ettie asked.

She shook her head. *"Nee,* I don't."

Now Ettie was intrigued. Since Florence would be with them at the library tomorrow, she'd have to look for a chance to have a quiet word with Ava and ask her to find—without Florence noticing—what she could about Wylie Morris, also known as Willis Gandara.

Chapter 6

The next morning, Ettie left Elsa-May and Florence outside the library while she hurried in front of them to talk with Ava alone.

Ava was sitting at a computer and looked up when she saw Ettie heading towards her.

"There you are. I thought you weren't coming."

"We had to reshuffle a few things to make time. Florence and Elsa-May are just outside. Before Florence gets here, I need to tell you something that I don't want you to let on to her."

"Okay. What is it?"

"I need you to find out about a singer called Wylie Morris. He was a popular singer back in the fifties. His real name is Willis Gandara. I don't know if his name had been changed legally or what. He was in jail for murder and he still could be doing time. I want you to find out where he is."

"And this has something to do with Florence?"

"Florence and he had a relationship many years

ago, but then he was accused of murder and went to prison. She then returned to the community, was baptized, and married an Amish man."

"And I'm guessing she won't be too happy if she knows we're finding out about a past lover?" Ava's eyes sparkled, obviously enjoying the intrigue.

"Exactly. She won't tell us anything about the murder he was accused of."

"Leave it to me. I'll let you know what I find out."

"Thank you." Ettie looked over her shoulder. "Here they come now."

After Ava greeted Florence, they all pulled up chairs to look at the computer screen.

"Now what am I looking up?" Ava asked.

Ettie unfolded her piece of paper. "I've made a list."

"Okay."

Ettie looked down at the page. "I need you to find out if there's any evidence that Dustin Gandara and Allissa Thomas knew each other."

"Ettie, he already said he didn't."

"We have to be certain, though, Florence."

"Okay, do what you have to do."

They both went to the same college?"

"Jah, that's right."

"She attended college—that's what it says here." Ava clicked through the images on Allissa's Facebook page.

"That's her?" Florence asked.

"Jah. All these photos are of Allissa Thomas," Ava said flicking through several images.

"That's him!!" Florence pointed to a group of people. "That's Dustin standing right next to her."

"Are you certain?" Ava asked.

"Of course I'm certain. Why would I say it if I wasn't?"

"Florence, that means he was lying to you. He did know her it seems," Ettie said.

"That doesn't mean he knew her," Florence said.

"Keep going, Ava," Ettie urged.

Ava flicked through more photos and found two more photos of Dustin and Allissa together.

Ettie shook her head. "It's not looking good."

"Are you able to print out those pictures for us, Ava?" Elsa-May asked.

"I can."

"Can you search to see if Dustin has a Facebook account?" Ettie asked.

"It's not likely. His name didn't come up when I hovered the mouse over his image and he wasn't tagged in any photos."

"We've got no idea what you're talking about." Elsa-May squinted at the screen.

"I'll search and see if he's on Facebook." Ava put Dustin Gandara's name into the search box. Many people had that same name, but none were the man they were after.

"He doesn't have an account," Ava announced.

"Are we going to mention to this to the police, Ettie?" Florence asked.

"They do their own investigations. They can, just as well as us, look this up. They've most likely seen this and it's harming him if he keeps saying he doesn't know her."

"I think we should tell his lawyer before the

police come across this information," Elsa-May said. "That is if they haven't seen it already."

"I'm sure they would've. This would be the first place they'd look these days," Ava said.

"Someone should tell, Dustin. We'll have to tell his lawyer," Ettie said.

Ava stood up. "I'll just get those photos off the printer." She came back and handed the photos to Ettie.

"Denke, Ava. We appreciate this."

"Let's see what the detective has to say, and make sure you hide those, Ettie," Elsa-May instructed.

"Okay," Ettie agreed. She tucked the photos down the front of her apron.

"I'll stay here and keep looking to see if I can find out anything else," Ava said.

"Gut!" Elsa-May gave a sharp nod.

As Elsa-May and Florence headed off to call a taxi, Ettie patted Ava on her shoulder. "Don't forget Florence is staying with us. I'll call you tonight to see if you found out anything else."

"Okay. I'll listen out for the phone."

"I think this young man is deceiving Florence. He says he has no knowledge of Allissa, but we can see from these photos that they knew each other. If there was just one photo, it might have been believable that he didn't know her, but going by all these photos, they must've known each other."

"It certainly looks like it," Ava agreed.

"And not only that, the forensic people found his DNA under her fingernails."

"It's not looking good, but it sounds as though your sister is very attached to this young man."

"Jah, she seems to be. Anyway, see what you can find out for me, Ava."

"Will do, Ettie."

Ettie hurried to catch up with her older sisters.

Chapter 7

Ettie and Elsa-May and Florence walked up the stairs of the police station. They came face-to-face with Detective Kelly as they walked through the door. Kelly had been talking to the officer at the front desk.

"There you are! Good timing. Come this way."

The three of them followed Detective Kelly through to his office.

"Did you find out anything, Detective?" Ettie asked, feeling guilty that she was hiding the photos underneath her apron.

"Yes, I got those two reports I was telling you about." He pushed a slip of paper towards Florence. "These are the two dates and the times that the gun was used in hold-ups."

"What were the names of the people who were killed, Detective?" Elsa-May asked.

"Why would you need to know that?" Kelly asked.

"It will help my sister if she happens to know them. After all, the gun was in her possession for years."

"We don't even know if it is the same gun. We have no proof that the gun used in these murders was ever in your sister's possession," Kelly said.

"It won't hurt to give us the names, will it?"

Florence added, "A simple search on the Internet would give us their names."

Ettie and Elsa-May stared at their sister who knew nothing about computers before their visit to the library earlier. She was certainly a fast learner.

Kelly reached over and took the slip of paper back. He looked at his file and then wrote the names down before he pushed the paper back toward Florence. "Happy now?"

"Yes, thank you."

"Ettie, we're looking into the possibility that these two victims had something in common."

"You are? Does that mean you think there might have been a connection?"

"In both robberies not much was stolen; each

seems almost like it was made to look like a robbery. It wasn't enough money to kill someone over."

"Will you let us know what you find out?" Ettie asked.

"I will if it will keep you all safe and out of this investigation. How's that?"

"That sounds good. Thank you," Florence said.

The detective stared at Florence. "Have a look at those dates, Mrs. Lapp, and see if they ring any bells."

Florence stared at the slip of paper. "It means nothing to me now. I'll need to go home and look in my notebooks. I keep detailed notes of what I did every day and who visited me."

"You do?"

Florence nodded.

"That's marvellous. If only everybody did that it would make my job a whole lot easier."

Florence chuckled.

"But didn't your notebooks burn in the fire?" Ettie asked.

Florence's face fell. "That's right. Everything was destroyed." She put a hand to her forehead. "Oh, what a bother."

"Yes, that does throw a wrench in the works. I was just about to suggest I could drive you all over there now and retrieve your notebooks." The detective shook his head. "I must be losing it. I knew you were staying at your sisters' place because your house burned down."

"We'll take Florence home and sit down with her while we go through her letters. She wrote to us about once a week. Maybe we can work out who visited her around those times. She often told us about who'd come to see her."

"Very good, Mrs. Smith. And contact me the moment you know anything," he said when he looked back at Florence.

"I certainly will."

"We've got a few errands to run now, but we'll be home after that. We'll be sure to call you as soon as Florence remembers something."

"Very good."

Chapter 8

"This looks to be a very old building. It makes me wonder if he's not a good lawyer," Florence said while looking up at the building where Claymore Cartwright's office was.

"He did a good job for some friends of ours," Elsa-May said.

"I'll have to take your word for that."

The three ladies walked up a few steps into the building, and then pushed the button for the elevator. They piled into the elevator and pushed the button for the fourth floor. When the doors opened, they stepped out.

Ettie looked around. The place looked the same as last time. All the other offices on that floor were still unoccupied.

Florence looked around, bewildered. "Has he moved?"

"*Nee,* he's up this way—at the end." Ettie led the way to the end of the corridor. She was pleased when she saw that his door was open. When she stepped through the doorway, the first thing she saw was his brightly colored baseball cap.

Claymore Cartwright looked up and bounded to his feet. "Hello there. I know you, don't I?"

Ettie stepped forward. "Yes, I'm Ettie Smith. We met before when you represented a friend, Jacob Esh."

"That's right, and this is your sister," he said smiling at Elsa-May.

"Yes, you've met Elsa-May, and this is another sister, Florence Lapp."

"Come in come in," he said as he arranged chairs for them in front of his desk. When they were all seated, he asked, "What can I do for you ladies?"

Ettie said, "We're here to see you about Dustin Gandara—he's been arrested."

"Oh, yes. He's my client."

"Yes, we found that out and that's why we're here," Elsa-May said.

Florence took over. "I was very close with his grandfather, and Dustin visited me a couple of times. He's a very nice young man."

"And you're here because…?"

"I heard on the wireless he'd been arrested."

"On the what?"

"She means the radio."

"I only listen to the news—nothing else. It was the day after my house burned down and I was staying with one of my daughters. Anyway, I visited Dustin and he insists he's innocent. What's more, when I talked to the police who arrested him, they mentioned a gun. When they described it, I knew it was my gun that they'd found."

Ettie pulled out the photographs from under her apron and pushed them toward the lawyer.

"Well," Florence said as Claymore flipped through the photos. "He claims he doesn't know this woman, but it appears he does?"

"Where did you get these photos?" he asked frowning.

"Off Allissa Thomas' Facebook page," Ettie said.

"Yes, I'm aware of these, and the prosecution

69

will no doubt have found them as well." He tossed them down on his desk.

"We thought perhaps you should tell Dustin that he should tell the truth," Elsa-May said.

"He insists he doesn't know the girl," Florence repeated her concerns.

"The photos prove it can't be."

"It can be, Mrs. Lapp. The fact is, that Dustin has a twin," Claymore said.

Florence gasped. "He didn't tell me that."

"According to Dustin, they don't get along," Claymore said.

"Well that must be it, then. The twin did it. They would have the same DNA, wouldn't they?" Ettie asked.

The lawyer shook his head. "They're twins, but they're not identical twins. Only identical twins have the same DNA. The two of them look similar, as any two brothers might, hence you mistaking them in these photos. They go to the same college, but they don't associate with one another."

"So we just need the twin brother to testify that

it was him in those photos to verify the fact that Dustin didn't know the girl?" Elsa-May asked.

"I'm working on it, but his brother has disappeared."

Elsa-May raised her eyebrows. "Doesn't that make him look guilty?"

The lawyer shook his head again. "His twin is not wanted for anything. There's no law against him disappearing. It wasn't his DNA under the girl's fingernails. The only problem might be if the prosecution claims they're photos of Dustin. Then I'll have to drum up some witnesses to say that the photos were of Darrin, the twin, and not Dustin."

"I wonder why he never mentioned he had a twin," Florence muttered.

Ettie raised her hand to get her sister's attention. "Could it have been Darrin who visited you and not Dustin, Florence?"

"It was Dustin in jail and he knew me too. What would be the purpose of Darrin seeing me; pretending to be his brother?"

"To get your gun?" Ettie suggested.

The lawyer raised both hands. "Can you tell me more about the gun, Mrs. Lapp?"

"The gun that they found in Dustin's car was Florence's gun," Elsa-May said before her sister could answer.

The lawyer frowned. "And do the police know that?"

Florence spoke quickly. "The police say that there's no proof it was my gun. But it's exactly the same gun. I saw a photo of it. They burned my house down and the gun was nowhere to be found. Dustin's grandfather gave it to me. He's the one who painted his initials on the gun and painted the trigger blue—for some unknown reason."

The lawyer tugged at his ear looking confused.

"I told the police that the gun has been with me for years. I checked every night to see that the gun was there, and there was no night that it was missing until the fire."

"And now your gun's gone missing?"

When Florence nodded, he made a couple of notes.

"My house burned down and the gun wasn't in the debris."

"That's interesting. When did the fire take place?"

"The day before Dustin was pulled over by the police for drunk driving."

The lawyer scribbled down some more notes. "Did you know that they've identified that this gun killed two people?"

Elsa-May nodded. "Detective Kelly said that."

"They're trying to find enough evidence to pin those murders on Dustin before we go to trial," the lawyer said.

"We were just at Detective Kelly's office and he gave us the names of the people and the dates they were killed. We are just going to go home and Florence is going to try to remember if she had any visitors on those particular dates," Ettie said.

"That's good, that's good. Can you give me your phone number, Florence?"

"I don't have a phone. I'm staying with Ettie and Elsa-May now. I stayed with one of my daughters,

Pearl, for a few days. I was at Pearl's when I heard about Dustin. One of my other daughters and her husband are arranging for my house to be rebuilt. Then I remembered how Ettie had a policeman friend and I thought he might be able to help." She lifted up her hands. "And here I am."

"He's a detective," Ettie corrected her sister.

"Do you have a phone, Mrs. Smith?"

"No, we don't," Elsa-May answered for her sister.

"Can you give me your address?" he asked.

Ettie gave the lawyer their address, and then asked, "Do you think Dustin's innocent?"

"It's my job to get him off. It's for the courts to decide whether he's innocent."

Ettie stared into his eyes waiting for him to say more, but he didn't.

"Okay, we should go. We've held you up long enough," Elsa-May said, pushing herself to her feet.

Chapter 9

They headed down the hallway and went down in the elevator.

"Well, he was certainly a surprise. I didn't expect a lawyer like him," Florence said.

"Jah, we were taken aback when we first met him. He's young and doesn't look like a lawyer, but don't worry, he wears a suit in court."

"That's good to know. As long as he does a good job it doesn't matter what his age is."

"What do you think about him being a twin?" Ettie asked.

Elsa-May frowned. "Claymore's a twin, too?"

Ettie sighed. "Not Claymore. I'm talking about Dustin being a twin."

"Ach, jah. That was a surprise."

"I wonder if there's any way that a twin can have the same DNA as the other one if they're not identical?" Florence said.

"The lawyer said 'no.' He'd be knowledgeable

about things like that," Ettie said.

"So the twin knew Allissa, but Dustin didn't," Florence said.

"That sounds perfectly reasonable to me. Seeing that the brothers never got along," Ettie said.

"How does Dustin get along with the rest of his *familye?*"

"Not well at all," Florence said.

"And you know why that is?"

"Nee, I don't. I'm only guessing, because he never spoke of them when he visited me. I only met him recently when he came to college nearby. He said he was going through his grandfather's things and found a letter I'd sent Morrie a long time ago. Dustin had my name and knew I was Amish, so he tracked me down. When he found out where I lived, he simply knocked. He said he wanted to meet someone who knew his grandfather. He was very proud of him."

"Why is he proud of him? Isn't his grandfather in prison for murder?" Ettie asked, trying hard to make sense of everything.

"That doesn't mean Morrie did it. Anyway, Dustin's proud of his grandfather's music."

"Did Dustin talk about him much? Where is Morrie now anyway?" Elsa-May asked.

Ettie asked, "Is he still in prison?"

"I told you before—that's something I'd rather not talk about," Florence said.

"Well, maybe next time you visit Dustin you can ask him about that. That is if you don't know where Morrie is."

"I have no intention of visiting Dustin again. I don't like prisons."

Elsa-May said, "I think you should visit him and ask him some questions."

"I'll consider it if you stop talking about it for a while."

When they were at home later that day, Ettie and Elsa-May pulled out all the correspondence they'd gotten from Florence over the years. Because she lived too far away for them to visit, that was how they'd kept in touch.

"These are all the letters from you," Ettie said as she placed the bundle on the kitchen table directly in front of Florence.

"And these are all mine," Elsa-May said.

Florence pulled the letters closer to herself. "It's a good thing I always put the date on my letters. Not everyone does that these days. Some letters come to me with just the day of the week."

"Elsa-May and I always thought it was funny that you didn't write to the both of us."

"I always wrote to you in turns."

"We read your letters aloud to one another," Ettie said.

"Now, we're looking for these dates." Florence tapped on the slip of paper the detective had given her.

Soon they had narrowed the letters down by timeframe.

"I just need to read these carefully to jog my memory."

"Do you want us to leave you alone?" Elsa-May asked.

"Jah. I need to relax and visualize what was going on in my life at that time. Make me a cup of tea, would one of you?"

"I've got to make a phone call. Maybe you can, Elsa-May?"

"I was just about to walk Snowy."

"Why don't I take him for a walk with me?"

"Okay," Elsa-May agreed.

Ettie grabbed Snowy's leash from beside the back door and clipped it onto Snowy's collar. "Come on, boy; you're going to go on a little walk with your Aunty Ettie."

Snowy looked up at her from his bed in the corner of the living room and wagged his tail before he hopped out of the bed and followed her to the front door. Together they hurried down the road.

Ettie popped some coins in the tin, and then picked up the phone's receiver. She dialed Ava's number, which was one of the phone numbers she remembered by heart.

"It's me, Ava. What did you find out?"

"Hello, Ettie. I found out that Morrie is still   in

jail waiting for parole."

"That's good to know. Did you find out what he was accused of?"

"Murder."

"I know, but do you have any details other than that?"

"Nee, I'm sorry, Ettie, I couldn't find any newspaper reports, but I didn't have a lot of time."

"Don't worry. I suppose that's not important at this stage."

"Ettie, I was thinking I could go to the college and ask around. I could talk with the friends of Allissa, the girl who was killed. I know who her friends are because she's got them all on Facebook. No one's closed her page down yet. She's still getting comments on her wall from mourners."

"That would be helpful if you could do that, but be careful."

"I could go tomorrow."

"That would be good."

"Okay."

"If this young man is telling the truth, how did

the DNA get under Allissa's fingernails?" Ettie asked. "That's one thing I can't get past."

"I've done a bit of research about DNA. There's such a thing as touch DNA. If you just touch something, you leave your DNA on it."

"Do you mean if someone shakes hands with me, and then with someone else later that day, my DNA could be left on their hands?"

"*Jah,* it's possible."

Ettie was silent for a moment.

"Ettie? Are you still there?"

"I'm thinking."

"Okay."

"Dustin claims he never met Allissa. I wonder if he touched something that she touched."

"*Jah,* but it wasn't found on the palms of her hands or her fingertips; his DNA was found under her fingernails. It sounds to me that she would've had to scratch him."

Ettie sighed. "Then why tell me about the other thing?"

"I just thought it was worth looking into."

"I suppose so. Just speak with her friends and see what you can find out. Oh, and wait. I forgot to tell you. Dustin had a twin, not an identical twin, but a twin who looked very much like him. We found that out when we went to see his lawyer."

"So that explains the photos?"

"*Jah.* The twin knew her and Dustin didn't. Apparently, the twins didn't get along. His name starts with a D too. I think it was Darrin.*"

"Good to know. I'm glad you told me that before I went to the college. So, this twin, I'm assuming he goes to the same college because he was in the photos?"

"I believe so. That's what the lawyer said."

"Is that all?"

"At this stage."

"I'll see what I can do, Ettie," Ava said before she hung up the phone.

Ettie replaced the receiver on the hook and then looked down at Snowy who was staring up at her. "Okay, okay. Let's you and I go for a little stroll. Don't you tell your *mudder* we were on the phone

82

for so long. That way, she'll think we had a nice long walk."

Snowy was sitting at her feet looking at her.

"Good boy. And when we get home, I'll find a special treat for you."

At the word 'treat,' Snowy stood on all fours and intently stared at her.

"I don't have one now. I said when we get home I'd give you one. Come on." Ettie walked down the road with Snowy beside her.

Ettie walked back into her house, crouched down and unclipped Snowy's leash. Snowy scampered to the kitchen and sat waiting for his treat. When it was slow in coming, he pawed at Elsa-May's leg.

"Get down, boy."

"Dogs should be kept outside," Florence said.

"That's exactly where he'll go in a minute if he doesn't stop bothering me."

Ettie walked into the kitchen. "I promised him a treat. That's why he's doing that." Ettie found him a piece of beef jerky and put him outside with it.

When she came back into the kitchen, she noticed that Florence and Elsa-May were unusually quiet. "Did you find out anything from the letters?"

"Jah, we found out that on those two dates I got visits from Linda and Reginald."

"Who are they?"

"Morrie and Reginald are brothers and Linda is Reginald's wife. They visited me a handful of times. But the last two times the dates were the very same as the ones when those two people were killed."

"The gas station holdup and the supermarket holdup," Elsa-May murmured.

"And are you sure they are the same dates?" Ettie asked.

Florence picked up two letters. "According to these, they are."

Ettie sat down. "So they're related to Morrie as well?"

"Jah."

"Hmmm. It gets more interesting." Ettie had thought it was odd that Dustin had visited Florence, but to hear that other relations of Morrie's had visited her made her more certain that Florence was right about someone burning down her house and taking her gun. Something wasn't right.

"What's our next move?" Florence asked.

"We'll need to tell Detective Kelly," Ettie said.

"Why don't I walk down to the telephone now and give him that information? We don't need to go there," Elsa-May said. "I haven't had my walk today."

"That would be *gut, denke,*" Ettie said.

"I'll take Snowy with me."

"He'll like that," Ettie said as Elsa-May walked out of the room.

Chapter 10

"They were in the same English Literature class," Ava informed Ettie over the phone the next day.

"So they did know each other? So Dustin must've known Allissa."

"Not necessarily. There were upwards of one hundred and fifty people in the class—it was a compulsory subject. But the interesting thing is that there was a reading list. One of the library books on the list was found in her bag when she died …"

"The library book?"

"Jah."

"Go on."

"There was only one copy of this book in the library and everybody had to read it, so everybody was told to be quick getting through it. I checked with the library and the person who had the book before her was Dustin. It's got a cloth cover, which is likely to grab DNA more readily than a plastic-covered book."

"I see, so that's how the DNA could've been transferred."

"Exactly!"

"Interesting."

"Also, I found out Allissa Thomas has—well, had— a very jealous boyfriend. He was possessive and violent. On one occasion, he hit her and she had a huge bruise on her face. None of her friends liked him. She broke it off with him only two days before she was murdered."

"I wonder what the detective will have to say about that. What was her boyfriend's name?"

"Andy Watkins."

"Andy Watkins. Okay, I'll try to remember that name."

"Have you learned anything further, Ettie?"

"The detective gave us the times that Florence's gun was used in two murders, and she had two visitors—the same two visitors on those two dates."

"That might be a coincidence. Someone   could

have broken into her house while she was out and then put the gun back when they'd finished."

"Do you know what intrigues me?"

"What's that?"

"The people who visited her were Morrie's brother and the brother's wife."

"So it all comes back to Morrie?"

"It does. Morrie knew Florence had the gun because he gave it to her."

"Guns aren't that hard to come by."

"But this one would've been hard to trace. Who would think of looking for a gun in an old Amish lady's house?"

"That's a point. Let me know if I can do anything else."

"Denke, Ava, I certainly will. You've been a marvelous help." Ettie hung up and then stared down at Snowy, who'd been sitting at her feet the whole time. She wondered whom she should give the information to first—the lawyer or the police.

She decided on the lawyer, and called for a taxi. She figured before it arrived she had enough time to get home and fill Florence and Elsa-May in on what Ava had found out.

"Let's go, and don't dilly-dally," Ettie said to Snowy.

Pushing the front door open, she called out to let both her sisters know what was going on, and then added, "I've called for a taxi. I'm heading to the lawyer to tell him what I've just told you. Do you both want to come with me?"

"I'll go with you," Florence said.

"*Jah,* me too," Elsa-May said.

* * *

Just as they were about to enter the building, they came face to face with Claymore Cartwright, who was on his way out.

"Hello again. You're here to see me?" he asked.

"Yes. Were you leaving?"

"I was just on my way out to grab a take-out coffee. Come upstairs and I'll make a call and have it delivered." He grabbed his phone from his pocket. "Would anyone like anything—tea, coffee?"

"We're good thank you," Elsa-May said.

"I'll have a white coffee with one sugar," Florence said.

"Good." He looked at Ettie.

"I'm fine, thanks."

He walked with them back to the elevator while he called the café on his mobile phone to make his order.

Once they were seated in his office, Ettie began to tell him all the information they'd gathered.

Claymore nodded. "I know the name—Andy Watkins. I know the police were originally looking at him as their prime suspect until the forensic report came back with Dustin's DNA."

"Tell him about the book, Ettie."

"It turns out that Dustin and Allissa were in the same class along with over one hundred other people. They had to read the same book. The book's still checked out under Allissa's name, and…."

Elsa-May interrupted, "And guess who read that

library book right before Allissa? Our friend told us something about touch DNA."

Ettie glared at Elsa-May. "Why did you ask me to tell him when you wanted to tell him?"

"You were speaking so slow I thought you'd never get it out."

"There were a couple of library books in her bag when they found her," Claymore said.

"It could've been one of those books," Elsa-May said.

Ettie continued, "Anyway, the book has a cloth cover. It's quite an old book and according to our young friend, that is a good way to transfer DNA from one person to another."

Claymore picked up a pen and tapped it on his desk. "I can use that, thank you; good work. I'll have my assistant go to the library and obtain a copy of their records."

Ettie turned around and looked at the empty reception area. "You have an assistant?"

"Yes, I do."

"Do you know anyone else who could have

wanted Allissa gone? Do the police keep you up to date?" Elsa-May asked.

"They do, but there's always a lag time, depending on what kind of information it is. I'm always happy to hear any ideas, or if you find out anything else don't hesitate to call me."

"When's this likely to go to trial?"

"I can't see it happening before six months."

"So, he's going to stay in jail for six   months?" Florence asked.

"Bail was denied. He doesn't have any strong family ties or ties to the community and the judge thought he was a flight risk. The evidence against him is pretty strong."

"Why would someone put that gun in his car?" Ettie asked.

The lawyer shook his head. "I have no idea."

"We've got something else to tell you. We found out that…" Elsa-May looked at Ettie. "Do you want to tell him, Ettie, or shall I?"

"You might as well go right ahead because you'd only interrupt me anyway." Ettie placed her hands firmly in her lap and pressed her lips together. She looked straight ahead while waiting on Elsa-May to speak.

"It's about the gun they found in his car. It was used in two robberies where people were killed."

Ettie couldn't stop herself from saying, "He knows that, Elsa-May."

Elsa-May ignored Ettie and continued, "On those very same days, our sister had two visitors and they were the same visitors each time."

Florence took over. "Yes, they were Morrie's brother, Reginald, and his wife, Linda. They got married in the seventies and have been together ever since. They visit me every so often, but not lately."

Claymore leaned forward. "And they visited you on the very days of those robberies?"

"On the very days. I have the letters to Elsa-May and Ettie to prove it."

The lawyer picked up a pen to write. "This Reginald, would he be Dustin's great-uncle?"

"That would be right."

"His grandfather's brother?"

Florence gave a nod of her head.

"And you know their whereabouts?"

"No, I don't. I think they said they live around Wilmington somewhere. I'm not sure whereabouts now."

"Their last name is the same as Dustin's?"

"That's right."

"And what was the nature of their visits?"

"Just to talk about old times."

"How long were their visits."

"Oh, hours. We had a lot to talk about."

"Could one of them have slipped into your bedroom without you looking?"

"I guess so. I remember Linda stayed there for a few hours on one of the visits while Reginald did some business in town."

"Have you told the police? I'm sure they'd like to hear this," the lawyer said.

"Do you want me to tell them? I don't want to get anybody into trouble."

"You should tell them."

"Okay, I will," Florence said.

"Can I have copies of those letters?" the lawyer asked.

"You can keep the letters if they'll help Dustin."

He nodded. "I think they will."

"Can I stop by tonight and collect them?" he asked.

"Of course."

Chapter 11

It was late in the day when they reached the police station.

They sat opposite Detective Kelly and told him what they'd learned.

"So what do you think about the book, Detective?" Ettie asked.

"The DNA was found under her fingernails. It's not my case. I have, however, offered my assistance to them."

"Did they tell you about the jealous boyfriend?" Florence asked.

"I read about him in the notes. Allissa had filed a complaint about him but then didn't go ahead with pressing charges. Are you certain that Dustin was the person who had the book before she did?"

"Yes. According to the library."

"How do you know that?" Kelly asked.

"My friend checked for me."

"Who? Ava?"

Ettie nodded. "Yes."

"I asked you to stay out of things."

"We did."

"I meant you and everyone else you know! I'm not happy that you've done this. You could all be charged for impeding an ongoing investigation."

"Could we?" Florence asked. "Would we go to jail for that?"

"You could."

Florence tipped her head to one side. "What's the accommodation like for women?"

"About the same as for men. Trust me, Mrs. Lapp, you wouldn't like it."

"Aren't you comfortable at our place, Florence?"

"It's fine, but there's nothing wrong with looking for an upgrade."

Ettie screwed up her face and turned to Florence. "I'm giving up my bed for you and you're considering going to prison because that's better than staying with us?"

"Not according to the detective."

The detective raised his hands. "Ladies, ladies.

Quiet! You can't go around sticking your noses into things. That's what I'm trying to get through to you. It makes things harder for the police to investigate."

"Okay," Florence said. "You shouldn't get so upset." She pointed to his head. "You have a pulsating vein in your forehead."

"You women will be the end of me. I can only try to help you with your friend, Mrs. Lapp, if you kindly restrain your sisters from investigating."

"Yes. I will. It occurred to me, though, that you might not be on the right side."

"What do you mean?"

"His lawyer is trying to get him off. Is that what you're trying to do?"

Detective Kelly frowned. "Yes, if he's innocent."

"Okay good. Phew!" Florence chortled.

"Are we all in agreement now, ladies?"

They looked at one another. "Okay."

"Now that I know you're on the right side, Detective Kelly, I can show you these letters. These letters prove that, on the same dates   those two men were killed in the holdups, on those very days, Linda and Reginald Gandara visited me."

Kelly leaned forward and took the letters from Florence's outstretched hand.

His eyes traveled quickly down one letter, and then the other. "I'd have to check my notes, but the dates here are clearly mentioned. On each occasion, you say you wrote to the specified sister the day after each of these visits?"

"Yes, when something happens I have something to write to my sisters about. I don't get many visits, except from my family, not many from *Englischers.*"

"Do you have a phone number or address for them?"

"Did I mention that Reginald is Morrie's brother?"

"Reginald is Wylie Morris' brother?"

Florence nodded.

"No, you didn't mention that. That is interesting. So it's more than likely that he knew you were minding a gun for his brother."

"Morrie gave me that gun—it was mine. He didn't give it to me to mind for him."

"What I mean to say is that he would've known you had a gun in your possession."

"Yes, it's possible he knew if Morrie told him," Florence said.

"Did you ever check the gun closely? Did you keep it loaded?"

"When Morrie gave it to me he said it was loaded. He showed me how to fire it. When I got married not long after Morrie went to jail, I kept it. I hid it in the attic of my house. It was only when my husband died and my children left home that I remembered it. From then on, I kept it under the bed, checking it every night—it's been there for many, many years."

"So, the bullets could've been spent and you wouldn't have known?"

"I suppose so, if someone took it away, used it, and then put it back where I had it."

"Are you certain you don't have an address for Linda and Reginald, or a phone number?"

She shook her head. "I don't. I asked for their address so I could write, but they said they move around all the time. They had one of those campervans and did a lot of traveling in that. I think they mentioned that they lived near Wilmington. They wouldn't give me a phone number because they knew I didn't have a phone."

"Thank you. I'll look into it. And I'll need a copy of the letters."

"The lawyer is coming tonight to pick them up."

Kelly raised his eyebrows. "I'll phone him and have him fax me copies."

"I didn't expect you to live in an ordinary house."

"What kind of house did you expect us to live in?" Ettie asked.

The lawyer gave an embarrassed laugh. "I thought you would live on a farm. I guess I'm showing my ignorance."

"We used to live on farms with our families," Ettie responded.

"But not a lot of Amish people live on farms any longer. A fair number still do, but they're being forced out due to the high price of the land," Elsa-May said.

He nodded. "Yes, the land prices keep going up and up."

"Come inside. Would you like a cup of tea?"

"Yes, good, thank you. Do you have any coffee?"

"Yes, we do. How do you have it?"

"Just black, no sugar."

He looked at the chair he was just about to sit on. "I've been looking for chairs like these. You don't want to sell them, do you?"

"You like them?" Elsa-May asked.

"I do, very much so. They have such craftsmanship." He ran his fingertips lightly over the carved backs.

"They're very old."

Ettie smiled. Now was the chance to get rid of the old chairs and buy some decent ones. "Well over one hundred years," Ettie added. "We could probably part with them to a good home. To someone who appreciated them."

"We couldn't possibly part with them. They've been handed down in the family." Elsa-May frowned.

"That's a shame," he said before he sat down. "A shame for me." He laughed.

Elsa-May stared at him for a moment before she disappeared into the kitchen to get him some coffee.

"How are things going with Dustin's case?" Florence asked.

"I'm still working on the case bit by bit. Do you have any other information?"

"No, we don't," Florence said.

Ettie wasn't listening. She was thinking of a way to get Elsa-May to agree to him taking the chairs away with him.

"Are you okay, Ettie?" Florence asked.

"Oh, I was just lost in thought. What were you saying?"

"Mr. Cartwright was just asking for the letters. You put them in a safe place?"

"Yes, I'll get them." As she pushed herself to her

feet, she said to the lawyer, "Detective Kelly has asked if you'd fax the letters to him."

"I can do that."

"Good." Ettie made her way to the kitchen.

"Are you here to help with the coffee?"

"Nee! I'm looking for those letters. I hid them in the cookie jar." Ettie unscrewed the jar. "Don't you think we should get rid of those old chairs and update the place? You've got to admit they're not comfortable."

"Nee, I like them. We don't sit on them."

"They aren't comfortable for our guests."

"I like to look at them. It reminds me of happy times when we used to go to *grossmammi's haus.*"

"*Jah,* they were in the dining room, not in the living room."

"What's the difference? Chairs are still chairs."

Ettie shook her head. She had to think fast while they had someone under their roof who liked the dreadful chairs. "Well, he mentioned buying them. We should at least ask how much he'd be willing to pay. Don't you think?"

105

Elsa-May turned and stared at Ettie with her mouth open. "You want to sell my memories."

"I do. Depending on how much."

"You're dreadful, Ettie."

"You are."

"Nee, you are! I'm not selling those lovely chairs. I don't see why you don't like them."

"You're so stubborn!" Ettie knew she was going about this all wrong, but couldn't think of any other approach that might work.

"You're the stubborn one!"

"They'll collapse on someone and then you'll feel bad." Ettie pulled the letters out of the cookie jar and stomped out of the room leaving the lid off the cookie jar.

"Here are both of the letters." Ettie handed the letters to the lawyer.

"Thank you." He put them in his inner coat pocket.

"Aren't you going to look at them."

"No, not right away. I'll look at them tomorrow. I try to switch off when I leave work. If I look   at them now, my mind will race and I'll have trouble sleeping tonight. It takes me some time to wind down after a day at work."

Ettie nodded, wondering how he could resist looking at them. What if they'd given him the wrong letters? Wouldn't he want to check on that, at least?

Chapter 12

As Ettie drifted off to sleep that night, she kept rethinking everything she'd learned over the past days.

It couldn't have been a coincidence that Morrie's brother and his wife had visited Florence on the exact two days of those shootings. It sounded like Reginald had taken the gun and then placed it back under her bed. And with Linda there to distract Florence, it wouldn't have been a hard thing to do.

It was a good thing that Ava found out about that library book that Allissa had borrowed directly after Dustin, but the DNA was found under her fingernails. Would that have been possible just by touching the same book? It seemed unlikely to Ettie.

The police had dropped suspicion of Allissa's violent boyfriend as soon as Dustin's DNA had been found. Another trip to the computer library to use the Internet was necessary to find out exactly where and when Allissa's body was found. No one had mentioned alibis. She knew Allissa's body was found on campus somewhere, but where? What was Allissa's boyfriend's alibi—did he have one? And what about Dustin?

It seemed like the police had targeted Dustin from the start, so they must've had a tip-off to ask for his DNA and search his car. From the way the police had acted, it certainly seemed like Dustin had been framed.

Ettie didn't want to get her sisters involved and decided she would slip away, and with Ava's help, gather more information.

The next morning, Ettie staggered out of the bedroom only half awake.

"Did you have a good sleep, Ettie?"

"Jah, I did, *denke.* How was yours?"

"Not too bad. The couch is quite passable, but of course, the bed is better."

"You can have it tonight," Ettie said. "Would you like some scrambled eggs?"

"Jah, I would."

"Me too please, Ettie."

Ettie turned to see Elsa-May walk into the kitchen.

"Have you already been for a walk?"

"Nee, we'll go after breakfast."

"I thought I might head into town today to run some errands."

"What kind of errands?" Elsa-May asked.

"Just go to the post office to buy some stamps, and things like that."

"Okay, that sounds *gut.* Florence and I will stay here in case the detective gets an update on anything."

"Oh, do you think he will?" Florence asked excitedly.

"He very often calls in on us when he has news," Ettie added.

"I hope he does, and soon. I can't believe those people were visiting me to use my gun." Florence shuddered. "It gives me shivers all over."

"It seems that's exactly what they did. What did

they talk about while they were there?"

"They talked about the old days. Reginald helped out with sound equipment. He came on tour with us. He was our—I forget the word for it now—the person who carries and sets up all the equipment. Anyway, that's what he was."

Ettie cracked eggs and then whisked them while listening to Florence talk about the old days when she was in love with Morrie. It was interesting to hear what they got up to since Ettie had always been in the community. She wondered if Florence's life was similar to the two of her daughters who had left the community.

After breakfast when Elsa-May came back from her walk, Ettie made her excuses to leave.

With Florence still in the kitchen, Elsa-May took hold of Ettie's sleeve just as she was heading out the door. "I know what you're doing."

"What's that?"

"You're seeing what else you can find out."

"I didn't want Florence to be involved."

Elsa-May chuckled. "It'll be easier for you to do

things alone. I'll keep her occupied, but only if you tell me what you find out when you get back."

"Of course I will. *Denke* for the help."

Ettie headed out the door, pleased that Elsa-May would keep Florence out of the way.

Once Ettie was down the road, she called Ava from the shanty and arranged to meet her at the library.

"Where are Elsa-May and Florence?"

"I thought it would be better if they stayed at home."

"Why?"

"Detective Kelly wasn't very nice when he knew you went to Dustin's college and asked questions."

"I suppose he wouldn't be."

"It's not his case. He said he's helping. Florence is convinced that her old boyfriend went to jail for a murder he didn't do."

"That would be dreadful if that's true."

Ettie told Ava about the letters and about the people who visited Florence on the same days the murders took place.

"Firstly, I need you to find out about Allissa's murder. Where it happened and if Dustin had an alibi. Then there was the jealous boyfriend—did he have an alibi?"

Ava asked, "What about Dustin's brother?"

"I forgot about him. Kelly said he disappeared, or maybe it was the lawyer who told me that. At any rate, the brother has gone and no one knows where he is."

"That seems odd."

"It does, especially when his brother's in jail—his twin brother. Surely he'd want to stick around and help."

"You'd think so. I'll write out a list. You want me to find out exactly where she was murdered and you want me to see what I can learn about Dustin's brother. What else?"

"Alibis. Did Dustin or Allissa's boyfriend have alibis?"

Ava said, "I don't know if I could find that out. Wouldn't that be in the police records?"

"Jah, but Kelly is being all funny about us being involved. He was very upset when he found out you'd been asking questions at the college. So I'd think he wouldn't want to tell us anything."

"I'll do what I can, Ettie, but there's only so much I can do."

"You can only do what you can do. Come over to the house later and let me know what you've found out."

"Okay, I will."

"Denke, Ava."

Chapter 13

There was a knock on the door and Ettie opened it to see Ava. She stepped back to let her inside. "Ava, come in, come in. What did you find out?"

Elsa-May came out of the kitchen. "It's nice to see you, Ava. Come through to the kitchen. We're just having a cup of tea."

Ava followed them into the kitchen.

Once they were all seated, Ettie spoke to her two sisters. "I asked Ava to see what else she could find out for me."

Florence's eyes opened wide. "And did you find out anything, Ava?"

"Not much. I heard that Allissa's boyfriend paid someone to say that he was with him at the time of the murder, but that could be just a rumor."

"It could be," Ettie agreed.

"Did you get a name, Ava?" Elsa-May asked.

"Yes, I wrote the name down. Oh, I left my notebook in the buggy. Do you want me to get it?"

"Nee, it won't mean anything to us. We'll have to find out if the police know what you've just told us."

"Did you find anything else out?" Ettie asked.

"That's all."

"I don't know what else we can do. I suppose we have to leave it up to the police.

At least he's got a good lawyer," Elsa-May said placing a cup of tea in front of Ava.

"Denke, Elsa-May."

Florence stared into the hot coffee before her.

"What if we think about what we know so far?" Ava suggested.

"Jah. Well, what do we know?" Florence asked.

"We know for certain that your friends visited each time the gun was used, Florence."

"But we don't know for certain that that's the same gun," Elsa-May said.

"Oh, Elsa-May, I know for certain that it's the same gun." Florence scoffed.

"Gut!" Ava said.

Ettie said, "Let's start there. It sounds to me like

it was Reginald who used the gun and then put it back later in the day after he'd used it."

Elsa-May said, "All right. Is everyone in agreement with that?"

Everyone nodded.

Ettie continued, "And if that's true, that means his wife was aware of what he was doing because she would've had to keep Florence busy while her husband used the gun."

Florence nodded. "That's true."

Elsa-May said, "I know what you're about to say next, Ettie. You're going to say why don't we pay them a visit?"

"We could, but Florence doesn't know where they live."

"I could get their address. If you know their names and the region they live my friend from DMV can get it," Ava suggested.

"You don't have to do that. I have their address," Florence said.

Ettie and Elsa-May stared open mouthed at their sister.

"But you told us you didn't know where they lived."

"I didn't want to tell the police because I didn't want to get them into trouble."

"I think they're in trouble right now. You've told the detective about them. They would've been tracked down and most likely already questioned," Ettie said.

"When shall we go?" Florence asked.

"Where do they live?" Ava asked.

Florence told Ava the address.

Ettie leaned forward. "And how would we get there?"

"Either by train or by bus," Ava said.

"Do you think we should? That detective friend of yours got awfully angry with you two," Florence said.

"Do you want to help Dustin or not?" Elsa-May asked.

"Of course I want to help him."

Ava said, "Are you sure you want to do this? If they've killed two people already, we can't go around and just simply ask them if they murdered people. How is this going to work—what's the plan? I don't want to get killed?"

"If you're nervous about it, Ava, you don't have to come with us."

"I think I do. I have to keep an eye on you two."

Florence giggled. "That rhymes—I *do,* I'll have to keep an eye on you *two.* "

When everyone looked at her stony-faced, Florence stopped laughing and straightened up clearing her throat.

Then, Ava drummed her fingers on the kitchen table. "Wilmington! I'll have to find the best way to get there."

"Linda told me it's a little over an hour by car."

"Well, we don't have a car," Ettie said.

"We could have Detective Kelly drive us," Elsa-May said.

Ettie scoffed. "He wouldn't do that in a million years. And besides that, he'll be angry that Florence lied to him."

"Did I lie? I think it wasn't a lie. I just didn't

offer up the address," Florence said. "I don't like to think that I lied about anything."

"What about old Detective Crowley? Last time we needed a car, he drove us," Elsa-May said.

"Nee, he offered to drive us. We can't call him and ask him to drive us somewhere when we haven't seen him lately. That'd be rude," Ettie said.

Ava nodded. "That's true."

"Then what?" Elsa-May asked.

"I've got a friend who might drive us," Ava said.

"Are you certain your friend would be willing to do that?" Ettie peered at Ava.

"I don't see why not. She's out of work at the moment and she was complaining about being bored."

"That might work. Of course we would pay for the gas," Elsa-May said.

"I can call her right now and ask." Ava looked around at all three sisters, who nodded. "When were you thinking of going?" Ava asked.

"How about tomorrow?" Florence suggested.

"The sooner, the better," Elsa-May said   while

Ettie nodded in agreement.

"Okay, I'll call her from the phone just down at the end of the road."

"Denke, Ava," Ettie said.

When Ava had left the house, Florence said, "I do hope we're doing the right thing."

Ettie stared at her sister. Now wasn't the time to be doubtful. "What are you thinking?"

Florence nibbled on a fingernail. "What if they burned my house down and killed those two people in the holdups?"

"They're your friends, Florence," Elsa-May said. "Do you think they'd be capable of something like that?"

"I don't know them that well."

"But you knew them well enough for them to visit you over the years."

Florence slumped down further in her chair. "I feel I don't know much about anything any more."

Elsa-May frowned at her sister and so did Ettie when she heard that Florence's voice had gone croaky.

Then tears formed in Florence's eyes. "Do you know what an awful feeling it was to come back home and find I had no home left?"

"I imagine it would've been an awful feeling," Elsa-May said.

"It's the worst feeling I've ever had in my life. The house was full of memories, full of all my clothes, and all my possessions. Everything I'd ever owned was destroyed. All I owned were the clothes I stood in and the barn."

Ettie felt bad now about being so prickly over giving up her bed every second night. She had a comfortable home and her sister had nothing.

"Did one of your daughters make you new clothes?" Elsa-May asked.

"*Jah,* and I had things given to me. But you know I've always been independent. I like to be the one doing the giving to others and not the other way around."

"You can stay here as long as you like," Ettie said.

Florence shook her head. "*Denke* for the offer,

but I won't stay here too long. Your house is far too tiny. I'll have mine rebuilt soon and then I'll be out from under your feet."

"You're not under our feet, Florence," Elsa-May insisted.

"I appreciate you both having me here. You two have always gotten along the best out of all of us sisters. I've often felt excluded by the both of you."

"I don't know about that," Ettie said.

"Nee," Elsa-May said to agree with Ettie. "It's just that our husbands died at roughly the same times and we sold our big farms at about the same time too."

"And yet here you are now, both living in the same house. You didn't write to me and ask me if I wanted to move here too. And don't say the place is too small. We could've all moved into a bigger *haus.*"

"I think your husband was still alive at the time when Elsa-May and I moved here."

Florence said, "All the same, it would've been nice to have the offer."

Ettie didn't know what to say, but saw that Elsa-May rolled her eyes.

Ettie blew out a deep breath. There was no pleasing some people.

Ava walked back into the house and came into the kitchen just in time to put an end to that topic.

"What is it, Ava? You look distressed."

Ava slumped down into the kitchen chair. "I've just got a lot going on lately."

"Did you find someone to drive us there tomorrow?" Florence asked.

"*Jah,* my friend, Holly. She said she'd do it."

"Oh, that's great."

"What time did you make it?" Ettie asked.

"I asked her to be here at nine o'clock. I mean, I asked her to come to my house at nine and then from there we'll come here to collect you three. Will that be all right? She doesn't wake up very early; she's gotten into a late routine since she hasn't got a job."

"I think that will be fine."

"We don't have to be there at any particular time."

"Now, what has you so flustered, Ava?"

"It's just that Jeremiah doesn't like me doing things like this and I don't like lying to him."

"What would you have to lie about?"

Ava gave a little giggle. "I don't know what I'm saying. I don't lie to my husband, but he's very single-minded about things."

"You mean closed-minded?" Florence asked.

Ettie and Elsa-May laughed.

Ettie said, "I think you've got it right there, Florence."

"He's just very intent on doing the right thing and that's one of the things I love most about him. Well, I better get home and break the news to him that I'll be spending the day with you tomorrow."

"Surely he'll be alright about that, won't he?" Ettie asked.

"Yes, I think he'll be fine."

"It's not as though we're going to be doing anything wrong or anything against the *Ordnung,*"

Florence said.

"Jah, I know that. I'll see you all tomorrow then."

Ettie walked Ava to the door. "We can forget the whole thing if something's bothering you."

"Nee, it's not that. I'm just a little tired and still adjusting to being married."

"Ah! Compromising."

"I guess that's what it is. Jeremiah and I are very different."

"You were older than most in the community when you got married. You've done a lot of things and you've lived by yourself. Most Amish women would have only lived with their families, and gone from there to being married. You've got your own ways now. There will be a time of adjustment."

Ava nodded. "I guess you're right. We have to learn to compromise on things."

"You do."

"Gut nacht, Ettie."

"Gut nacht, Ava."

Ettie leaned against the door and watched Ava

get into her buggy. When Ava was seated, she waved to Ettie and Ettie waved back. It was nice to have a young friend to remind her of what it was like to be young. When Ava drove away, Ettie rejoined the others.

"Did your friend not want to do it? Is that why she had a sad face?" Florence asked.

"*Nee,* she's fine," Ettie insisted.

Chapter 14

Ettie woke up on the couch the next morning to Snowy licking her face.

"Get off!" She pushed Snowy away and when she sat up, she placed him on the floor.

Elsa-May walked toward her. "What's the matter?"

"Snowy! He was licking my face."

Elsa-May giggled. "Sorry about that. Do you want me to have him sleep outside tonight?"

"No, because tomorrow morning Florence will be sleeping here." Ettie chuckled.

"That's mean," Elsa-May said.

"I thought I was being kind to Snowy letting him sleep inside."

Elsa-May said, "I know what you're playing at."

"What time is it?"

"It's still early. We've got a couple of hours before Ava's friend gets here."

"Is Florence awake?"

"She's snoring her head off."

After Ettie had pulled on her robe, she headed to the kitchen to boil a pot of water for her usual morning cup of hot tea.

"Would you like pancakes for breakfast?" Elsa-May asked.

"I'd love some," Ettie said.

"Should we let Florence sleep or should we wake her up?"

"Let her sleep while she's in my bed. The couch isn't that good."

"I thought you said it wasn't too bad."

"You can't spread out, other than that, it's alright." Ettie whispered to Elsa-May, "The only reason Florence thinks that the boy is innocent is because she was once in love with his grandfather."

Elsa-May whispered back, "It's a very real possibility he might be guilty. And I think we have to keep that in mind."

Ettie nodded. She had been swayed by her

sister convincing her that Dustin was innocent, but the reality was that Florence hardly knew this boy. The relationship that she'd once had with the young man's grandfather... Ettie bit her lip when she remembered that the grandfather had been convicted of murder. A murder that Florence refused to tell them about!

While Elsa-May cracked eggs for the pancake batter, Ettie stared off into the distance wondering why Florence was being so secretive. If she wanted their help, the least she could do was to be forthright with them.

Elsa-May whisked the pancake mixture with a wooden spoon. "Ettie, the water's boiling."

"Oh, that didn't take long. Cup of tea?"

"Jah, I will thank you."

"I'd like to find out more about the murder Morrie was convicted of."

"Why? Do you think that has something to do with his grandson?"

"I don't know it just makes me uneasy that Florence isn't telling us about it."

"She might simply think it's none of our business. Which it really isn't."

"What are you two whispering about?"

They looked behind them to see Florence.

"You're awake!" Elsa-May said.

"We just didn't want to wake you," Ettie said. "Tea?"

"Jah, denke." Florence pulled her dressing gown tighter around her and sank down onto one of the chairs at the kitchen table.

"Are you okay with pancakes for breakfast?" Elsa-May asked Florence.

"That's fine. Everything's okay. Are we late?"

"Nee, we've got plenty of time."

"Gut!"

"How was the bed?"

"It was fine. Better than the couch."

When Ettie placed a cup of hot tea in front of Florence, she had to bite down on the inside of her lip to stop herself from asking questions about Morrie. She reminded herself to wait for a better time.

"That'll be Ava!" Ettie called out from her room later that morning when she heard a knock on the door. She had just placed her prayer *kapp* on her head over her fastened braids. Because Ettie had been left to do the washing up, she was the last to be ready. She tied her apron around her waist, and hurried out to join the others.

"Hi, Ettie. They're getting in the car," Ava said.

It appeared Ava was the only one in the house.

"Is there room for all of us?"

"Jah, there's plenty of room."

Ettie closed the front door behind them and headed to the car. Her sisters were involved in a discussion outside the car.

"I'll get in first," Elsa-May said.

"Nee, that'll mean I'll be in the middle," Florence said, placing her hands firmly on her hips.

"Someone has to be in the middle," Elsa-May said while getting into the car.

Florence turned and looked at Ettie. "You get in next, Ettie."

"Nee, I don't want to sit in the middle either."

Ettie saw that Elsa-May was now sitting smugly by the far window.

"Neither do I."

"I'll sit in the middle," Ava offered. "One of you can sit in the front.

"*Nee,* Ava, you sit in the front with your friend, I'll sit in the middle." Ettie got into the car and when they were all in with the doors closed, Ava got into the front seat and introduced them to her friend.

"It's very good of you to do this, Holly," Elsa-May said.

"I'm happy to do it."

Florence handed over some money. "This should cover the gas."

"Thank you." Holly took the money and put it in the glove box. "Buckle up." Holly turned and looked at them.

"We're all buckled up," Florence said.

Ettie looked at Florence. "You haven't done yours."

Florence glared at Ettie while fumbling for her

seat belt strap. "I was just about to do it. You'll have to move over so I can clip it in."

Ettie moved closer to Elsa-May while Florence clipped her seat belt on.

"We all good now?" Holly asked looking in the rear-view mirror.

"Yes," Florence said.

"Do you know how to get there, Holly?" Ettie asked.

"Yes, I've got GPS."

Ettie raised her eyebrows wondering what she was talking about. Ava turned around and explained to the three elderly sisters what GPS was while they drove off.

"How long will it take?" Florence asked.

"According to the GPS, we'll be there in one hour and twenty minutes," Holly said.

"Good, that's not too far," Ettie said.

Chapter 15

With some unexpected slow traffic holding them up, they eventually arrived at Reginald and Linda Gandara's house one hour and fifty-five minutes later.

"Ava, you and Holly stay in the car. We don't know what we'll be facing," Elsa-May said.

Ava frowned. "Are you going to be in danger?"

"No, these people are my friends," Florence insisted.

When Florence and Elsa-May got out of the car, Ettie leaned over, and asked in a quiet voice, "Have you got a mobile phone, Holly?"

"Yes, I have."

Ettie tapped Ava on her shoulder. "Don't hesitate to call 911 if something looks odd."

"You can't do this…"

"We'll be okay. I'm just saying that as a precaution." Ettie got out of the car to join her sisters.

Elsa-May and Florence stood together at the front door while Ettie stayed behind them. Florence pressed the doorbell and within seconds the door was flung open.

"Oh, my golly! It's you, Florence!" An elderly lady leaned forward and kissed Florence on each cheek.

Ettie knew it must be Linda, but somehow she'd been expecting someone younger. She had fair hair that fell about her shoulders in waves. It was a style appropriate to someone younger, in Ettie's opinion.

"What are you doing here?"

"Hello, Linda. These are two of my sisters."

Once everyone was introduced, Linda said, "Come inside. I couldn't believe it when I looked out the window and saw Amish women. Then I thought one of them might be you, Florence. Is everything okay?"

"Everything's fine. I'm here to ask you a couple of questions."

She laughed. "Sounds ominous. Come and   sit

down."

Ettie remained silent and sat down with the rest of them.

"Where's Reginald?" Florence asked when she'd sat.

"He's out of town at a friend's funeral. I didn't want to go, so I stayed home."

"Linda, I'll be blunt and come right to the point of the visit. Two of the times you visited me, two people were killed in armed holdups and my gun was used. I'm thinking that Reginald took the gun from under my bed, and used it in these robberies and killed those two people. The police know all about it."

"The police know? What do they know?"

"It's only a matter of time before they knock on your door," Elsa-May said.

"People were killed?" Linda asked, looking shocked.

"On each occasion one person was killed, making two in total," Elsa-May said.

Linda shook her head as tears came to her eyes.

"I didn't know anyone was killed."

"You knew about the robberies, though?" Elsa-May asked.

"Yes, I did. Oh, this is awful. We were so broke." She looked at Elsa-May, and asked, "Have you ever been broke?"

Elsa-May nodded. "I have—very much so."

Linda continued, "We hadn't been that short of money for literally years. It's an awful feeling."

"I thought you were wealthy. You've got that huge campervan and everything," Florence said.

"We've got many debts. We don't own the van. We needed the money. He said he knew an easy way to get money and it wouldn't be traced back to us. At first, I didn't know how he got the money, but I knew he most likely stole it from somewhere. It was only a few hundred dollars a time. Later on, he told me he stole the money from places that didn't have CCTV cameras."

"I think he must've been wrong about that," Ettie said.

"You haven't had a visit from the police yet?"

Elsa-May asked.

Linda gasped and her eyes widened. "He's been caught on tape? Do you think that's how they know he did it?"

Elsa-May persisted. "The police haven't come to arrest him yet?"

"No, they haven't."

"If you come forward and tell the police, they'll go easy on you, I'm sure," Elsa-May said. "But you might have to get in first and tell them about your husband. I think that's how it works."

"Do you think so? What will happen to him?" Linda asked.

Ettie was pretty sure Linda knew exactly what had gone on even though she claimed to have no knowledge of the murders—only the robberies.

"They'll most likely go easier if you come forward and admit everything you know," Elsa-May said. "It's only a matter of time before they arrest him, and maybe you too."

"You could be charged as an accessory to murder and covering up a crime—two crimes," Ettie said.

"Why don't we call our Detective Kelly and have him work some things out?" Elsa-May suggested.

"Yes, Linda, my sisters have a good friend who is a detective. He'll help you."

Linda nodded. "Thank you. I appreciate you going to all this trouble for me. I can't believe he killed two people. I had no idea. You believe me, don't you, Florence?"

"If that's what you say, then I believe you," Florence said.

"I didn't know. I only knew about the gun and that he wanted to use it to get money."

"How did you know that Florence had a gun?" Ettie asked.

"Reginald found out from his brother."

"Did you have my house burned down?" Florence asked, now frowning.

"What? I didn't even know your house was burned down. How could you think I could do such a thing?"

Florence shook her head. "I don't know what to think any more. The gun was missing—it wasn't found after the house burned down. The firemen said that it wouldn't have been destroyed and it wasn't found."

"I didn't have anything to do with it."

"Another thing you mightn't know, seeing you haven't mentioned it since we've been here, is that Dustin has been arrested," Florence said.

"Yes, we heard about it."

Ettie stared at Linda. She didn't seem too upset that her husband's grandnephew was in prison. Ettie stood up. "Can I get myself a glass of water?"

"Yes, of course. The kitchen is straight down there."

Ettie had suddenly remembered about Dustin's brother—the missing twin. Since Darrin was also related to Reginald Gandara, there was a chance he might have been staying with him and Linda.

Chapter 16

Before Ettie entered the kitchen, she looked round for any signs that Darrin might be staying in the house. She looked back over her shoulder to see Linda busily talking to her sisters.

Trying to be as quick and quiet as she could, Ettie climbed the stairs. When she got to the top, she peeped into each bedroom. In one of the rooms, the bed was unmade, there was a small television on a table by the bed, and a laptop computer was plugged into the wall. *They certainly have someone staying with them,* Ettie thought.

Ettie went back down the stairs and joined the others.

"She's agreed to let us call Detective Kelly," Elsa-May said to Ettie.

"Yes, but I must make a phone call first," Linda said standing up and reaching for her mobile phone on the coffee table.

Ettie sat down. There was nothing they could

do to stop Linda from making that call. Was she calling her husband to warn him and tell him to make a run for it, or telling her grandnephew not to come back to the house?

Linda walked out of the room to make the call.

Elsa-May glanced out the window. "I hope Ava and her friend don't mind waiting in the car."

"They'll be fine," Florence said.

Ettie leaned forward and told Elsa-May that there was a possibility that Darrin was staying in the house.

"What?" Florence asked.

Elsa-May leaned over and whispered what Ettie had just told her.

Five minutes later, Linda sat back down. "Okay, call this detective you know." Linda passed her phone to Ettie who handed it to Elsa-May.

"You call him, Elsa-May."

"I don't know his number off the top of my head."

Ettie told her the number and after Elsa-May had pressed the numbers into the phone, she stood.

When she got through to the detective, she told him where they were and that Linda Gandara had some vital information to tell him about her husband and the gun that had been kept at Florence's house.

When Elsa-May ended the call, she sat back down.

"What did he say?" Linda asked.

"He said he'd be right over and asked if we would stay put."

Ettie breathed out heavily. "We've got friends waiting in the car."

"You must have them come inside, Ettie. I'm sorry, I didn't realize. You get them and I'll fix us something to eat."

Ettie went out to the car, while Linda headed to the kitchen. Ava, Holly, and Ettie came inside. As soon as they'd sat down, they heard a car. Ava jumped up and looked out the front window. "Is that your friend?"

Florence was the first to make it up off the couch to look out the living room window where there was a clear view of the road. "She's doing a runner!"

"Ach nee! Kelly will blame us. Quick, Elsa-May, call him again and tell him what just happened."

"Can you see her plate number?" Elsa-May asked.

"Nee, but they'll find it quickly once they know their names and address," Ettie said.

Elsa-May was quickly making the call. She was able to give him Linda's last dialed numbers because Linda had fled without her mobile phone.

Kelly asked them—again—to stay put until he arrived.

"What's going on?" Holly asked.

"Was that Linda driving off?" Ava asked.

"Yes, we've called the police and they're coming here right now. Detective Kelly told us to stay put."

"How exciting!" Holly said.

"Perhaps she found she didn't have any coffee, so she's driven down to the shop to get some?" Florence suggested. Then Florence giggled. "Wouldn't we look silly if that's all she was doing?"

Ettie shook her head. "That's not likely by the

speed she took off at."

Holly said, "She's done a runner for sure."

Ettie and Elsa May stared at each other and Ettie knew they had the same thought. They were going to be in terrible trouble with Detective Kelly. They would have to sit and listen to him reprimand them for going to see Linda rather than giving him Linda and Reginald's address.

And for the first time, Ettie would have to agree with him that giving Kelly their address would've been a better idea. They'd done a silly thing. Linda had openly admitted that her husband had taken that gun to rob people. They all could've been in harms way, even Ava and Holly who'd stayed in the car.

"I wonder if Reginald will come home?" Florence said.

"Not for a while," Elsa-May said. "His number was one of the numbers Linda called before she left."

The five of them sat in the living room waiting for the detective

"This is quite exciting. It beats staying home watching the TV all day," Holly said.

Seeing the worried look on Ava's face, Ettie asked, "Are you worried about what Jeremiah will say?"

"I am. If I'm late getting home, I'll have to tell him where I was. He's already asked me not to get too involved with you when you help the detective."

"If it comes to that, I'll have a talk with him," Elsa-May said. "But we shouldn't be home too late. It's not that far."

"Thank you, Elsa-May, he listens to you."

Ettie turned to face Florence. "So Dustin didn't mention he was a twin on any of his visits?"

"Nee, I already told you I didn't know. I last saw his, Dustin's father when he was a boy of about seven. I never kept in touch with any of Morrie's family. Why would I?"

"I don't know, but then again, you've hardly told us much about Morrie at all," Ettie said.

Florence pursed her lips looking none too happy.

Then they heard cars come screeching to a halt. They all stood to see Detective Kelly's car pull up at the house followed by two police cars.

He got out of the car and hurried to the door and Ava opened it before he reached it.

"Is everybody okay?" he asked as he hurried inside.

"Everybody's fine," Ava said.

"They've caught Linda and they're taking her in for questioning."

"Great! They've got her?" Holly asked.

The detective stared at Holly. "Who are you?"

"She's a friend of mine," Ava said.

Detective Kelly nodded and then sat down as four uniformed police officers made their way through the house

"Tell me everything," he said. "Tell me exactly what happened."

"It was my idea," Florence said.

"So you did have their address after all?" Kelly glared at Florence.

"Yes, I did, but I didn't want to get anybody   in

trouble. That's why I kept it to myself."

"Just tell me what happened and please try to remember everything Linda said to you."

They gave Kelly Linda's cell phone and then told the detective everything about their visit.

"Don't they need to have a warrant or something?" Holly asked as everyone watched the police officers take a laptop and a computer out of the house.

"They were about to be served with a warrant today," Kelly said.

"They were?" Florence asked.

"Yes, it seems his van was caught on CCTV leaving the scene of both crimes."

"His big campervan?" Florence asked.

"Apparently so. I'm afraid you're going to have to give statements."

"Even me?" Holly said.

"Yes, everyone in this room will need to give statements."

Ava held her stomach. "But we've already just told you everything we know."

"Yes and you're going to have to repeat it all in your official statements."

"How exciting!" Holly said once more.

"Now do you believe me about the gun being the same as the one at my home?" Florence asked Kelly.

"Yes, it seems likely," Kelly said.

"What I'd like to know is why they had to burn down my home!"

"Hopefully, we'll find that out in due course."

"Linda admitted that her husband used my gun and then put it back."

Kelly nodded. "I think you should save your talk now for when you're interviewed."

Once everyone was in the car, they followed Kelly back to the police station, closer to home and the one where Dustin had been arrested. After they had all made statements, Holly drove them home.

It was well after dinnertime when the three elderly sisters walked through the door. They'd stopped to get takeout burgers on the way home. Holly had taken Ava home first because they were all concerned about being late and having Jeremiah arrive home to no Ava and no dinner.

"I sure hope Jeremiah likes burgers," Ettie said as they sat down to eat their burgers at the kitchen table.

"I'm sure he would," Elsa-May said.

"If he doesn't, he should stop being so fussy!" Florence said as she unwrapped her burger.

Elsa-May broke off a piece of burger and gave it to Snowy, who was sitting at her feet.

"That was an exhausting day," Florence said.

"Florence, how easy is it to get in and see Dustin?"

"You have to call and book the visit. They'll let you in to see him and talk with him through a screen, but it'll be a non-contact visit."

"What are you thinking, Ettie?"

"I'm thinking of going to see him."

Elsa-May tipped her head to one side. "Really?"

"Jah. Why not?"

Elsa-May raised her eyebrows. "Okay. What will you ask him?"

"I've got a list of questions." Ettie tapped her head. "It's all up here."

"I'll have to come with you. He doesn't know you."

"*Jah.* Shall we do it?"

Florence's eyes twinkled. "I think we should."

Chapter 17

The next afternoon, Ettie and Florence arrived at the prison by taxi. They had been told to be there for security screening one hour prior to their booked visit.

"It's intimidating," Ettie said looking up at the double-wired fences with layers of rolled barbed wire across the top.

"It gets worse," Florence whispered as they proceeded further.

Once they were through to the visitors' gates, they gave their names at the desk. There were four armed-guards standing near them. Then they joined other visitors who were sitting, waiting.

Ten minutes later, a German Shepherd with a prison guard holding his leash walked up to them. "Don't touch the dog!" the guard ordered.

The dog sniffed each person, heading down the row.

Then everyone was ordered to move to another

area. On the way there, they were escorted by two armed-guards.

"I feel like I've done something wrong," Ettie whispered to her sister.

Florence whispered, "It certainly makes you feel that way."

They came to another section where they had to take their shoes off and place them into a basket to be x-rayed.

"What's this for? I thought you said it was a no-contact visit," Ettie said.

"It is. But they x-ray the shoes and then we have to walk through a scanner."

Ettie pulled a face. It was certainly a process just to visit someone. Now Ettie knew why they had to be there an hour before. Once they walked through the scanner, they were allowed to put their shoes back on.

They were then directed to booths and told to wait.

"More waiting?"

"It won't be long now," Florence whispered

back.

"Will he be able to hear us?"

"Jah." Florence nodded.

Five minutes later, a row of prisoners filed past them. Then a young man was directed to their booth by a guard.

He sat down and smiled at Florence. "Thanks for coming again."

"My pleasure. This is my sister, Ettie. She's helping your lawyer to get you off."

"You are?"

Ettie nodded.

"Thank you. I'm glad you believe me."

Ettie shook her head. "I don't."

Florence gasped. "Ettie!"

Dustin opened his mouth, but no words came out.

"You lied about knowing Allissa," Ettie said.

When he remained silent, Florence looked at him, and said, "You must tell the truth if you want our help."

He leaned forward. "I was scared; that's why I

said that I didn't know her. I didn't really know her, I just saw her at school, but I spoke to her once and that was just before she got killed."

"Is that why you lied—because you thought you'd be blamed?" Florence asked.

Ettie dug her sister in the ribs. She didn't want her to influence what Dustin was telling them. He'd lied once, so it'd be easier to do it again. "Keep going, Dustin."

Dustin looked at each of the two women in front of him, and then looked down.

"What did you say to her?" Ettie asked.

He looked at Ettie. "I told her to stop stringing my brother along. He was in love with her and she was using him and she had that idiot boyfriend."

Ettie asked, "What did she say?"

"Nothing! She slapped me across the face and told me it was none of my business. She yelled at me and told me my brother was a stalker. Then I left."

"Where did you go?" Florence asked.

"That explains it," Ettie said.

"What?" Dustin asked.

"The DNA under her fingernails. She slapped your face?"

He nodded.

"Why didn't you tell anyone?" Florence asked.

"I did! I told the police, but they didn't listen."

"Did you tell your lawyer?" Ettie asked.

Dustin shrugged his shoulders. "He thinks I'm guilty, so what does it matter?"

"You'll have to tell your lawyer," Florence said.

"Why did you go out of your way to help your brother when you don't get along?" Ettie asked.

"He's a total jerk, but he's still my brother."

Ettie and Florence stared at each other.

Dustin continued, "No matter which way you look at it, there's no proof that I didn't do it. The police need to find the person who did it. That's the only way I'll get off the charges."

"You should've told the truth from the start." Florence shook her head.

"I did! As far as I could, I did. I didn't know what was going on and didn't even know they'd searched my car and found that gun until I was at the bail hearing."

Florence gasped. "I thought you told me you saw them find the gun when they pulled you over?"

He shook his head. "I knew nothing about the gun. I only saw it at the bail hearing. I thought I'd been arrested for DUI. I didn't know they were charging me for Allissa's murder, and then they talked about the gun they'd found. They had the gun there as evidence and that's the first time I'd ever seen it. They said I had it hidden in the car."

"We still don't know who killed Allissa," Ettie said.

Florence leaned forward and whispered to Dustin, "Don't you worry, Dustin, Ettie has a nice policeman working hard to get you out."

"Really?"

He looked relieved, but Ettie was worried about him having false hope. "We're doing all we can."

"Thank you, Ettie."

Ettie smiled at him and in that moment she too believed that he was innocent.

A bell rang, signifying their visit had come to an end. They stood up at the same time as Dustin. A large prison guard stood next to Dustin and walked away with him.

Ettie looked at her sister who looked as though she would cry. "Don't worry; something will come to light to get him off."

"He's still in jail even after Linda admitted Reginald was the one who used the gun."

"I know, but at least Dustin will be cleared of those two murders. Now we just have to have him cleared of the charges for Allissa's murder."

"Well, let's do it."

Ettie looped her arm through her older sister's and together they walked to the exit while being glared at by two heavily armed prison guards and one serious-looking German Shepherd.

"We're slow because we're old," Ettie said trying to lighten the moment as they shuffled past the guards. It didn't work; none of the guards changed their stony expressions.

Once they were outside the gates, Florence

looked at the prison. "What a dreadful, dreadful place."

"It is. We have to get him out of there." Ettie glanced back at the huge wire fence with the twisted barbed wire on top. "It was bad enough being a visitor. I felt guilty. I probably would've admitted to a crime if they'd questioned me—out of fear alone."

Florence tugged at her sister's sleeve. "We still don't know who burned my house down and the police haven't found out who really killed Allissa. It makes sense that it was Linda and Reginald who burned down my house because of the gun. What do you think?"

"If they'd taken it before, why not just take it again? Why destroy your home?"

"I don't know," Florence said as they walked closer to one of the three waiting taxis.

"I'm going to call Detective Kelly and ask him to come for dinner. Perhaps if we put our heads together, we can find something we've been missing."

"Do you think so, Ettie?"

"That's what I'm hoping. We have to call Dustin's lawyer and tell him what Dustin told us. It might get him off because now we know that the DNA got there because Allissa slapped his face. And that explains the marks on his face in his arrest photos."

"We'll head to the first public phone box and call him from there."

"Let's go home first and make sure it's okay with Elsa-May."

Chapter 18

When they got home, Ettie told Elsa-May about her idea of inviting Kelly to dinner.

"What does he like to eat?"

"Fast food."

"I know that, but we can't feed him that. What else does he like?"

"He probably is like most men," Florence said. "He likes anything that he doesn't have to cook himself."

Elsa-May and Ettie looked at each other.

"Elsa-May, what were we having for dinner tonight?'

"I was just going to make us cabbage soup."

"Really? What else do we have that we could cook?"

"We could make a lamb roast with roasted vegetables."

"*Jah,* I think he'd like that more."

"Call him now, Ettie, before he makes   plans,"

Florence urged.

"Okay, I will." On the way to the front door, Ettie saw that Snowy was fast asleep. She took money for the call from the jar on the table near the entrance and stepped outside. A cool breeze blew over her as she continued down the front steps of her house.

On the way to the shanty, she replayed everything in her mind. The mystery was like a giant puzzle, they had some of the pieces, but the other pieces were missing or didn't fit. Hopefully Kelly would offer some information while he was relaxing over dinner.

Ettie picked up the receiver, and then dialed Kelly's cell phone number.

"Detective Kelly."

"Oh, it's you?" Ettie asked.

"Mrs. Smith?"

"Yes, it's me. I didn't expect you to answer."

"You called my mobile phone."

"Okay."

"What can I do for you?"

"Elsa-May and I were wondering if you'd care to join us for dinner tonight."

"Tonight?"

"Yes, tonight. If you can't make it, what about tomorrow night?"

"Tonight suits me. Thank you, I'll look forward to it."

"Good, good."

"What time would you like me to be there?"

"How does six sound?"

"That's a little early for me."

"Seven?"

"That's better if that's not going to put you out."

"Seven will be fine. We'll see you then."

"Very good."

Ettie hung up the phone, pleased that one part of her plan had worked. The other part was that Kelly would tell them some information that would help to free Dustin Gandara. Or at least help them figure out who had placed the gun in his car. They already knew why; it had to be to implicate Dustin, but who would want to see harm come to him?

Ettie headed back to the house. She had a few ideas swirling in her mind.

"He's coming! He said he could come for dinner." Ettie squealed as she walked in the door.

Elsa-May came out of the kitchen. "That's great."

"He said he'd be here at seven."

"Okay. I'll start preparing it."

Ettie sat back down at the kitchen table with Florence. "I know you only met Dustin a handful of times, but did he mention having any enemies?"

"*Nee.* He talked about his grandfather and his music. He didn't talk about personal things about himself. I told him stories about the old days and that's about it."

Ettie nodded.

Chapter 19

It was five minutes past seven and Ettie was growing concerned that something important had cropped up and Kelly wouldn't make it for dinner. Having no phone in their house, Kelly wouldn't be able to give them the courtesy of telling them he'd be late or wouldn't be able to come at all.

Just then, Ettie heard a car and looked out the window. It was Kelly's car. "He's here!" she announced to Elsa-May and Florence.

Ettie made her way to the door, opened it and waited for Kelly to approach. She thought it best to keep quiet about her visit to the prison. As long as the lawyer had the information they'd learned—that was the important thing.

When Detective Kelly stood in front of her, he said, "Good evening. That smells delicious. I could smell it as soon as I got out of the car."

"Hello, Detective. Come inside."

"Thank you." He stepped past her into the house.

Snowy ran at him and jumped up at him.

"Stop it, Snowy," Ettie said trying to push him away lightly with her foot.

The detective held up his leg. "Can you get him off me?"

Ettie scooped Snowy up. "The others are in the kitchen."

He nodded and headed to the kitchen while Ettie put Snowy in the yard and put the latch over the dog door. After that, she joined them in the kitchen.

"I'll just wash up and join you in a minute."

Elsa-May looked up from dishing the food onto the plates. "Well, don't be long."

When Ettie got back to the table, she sat down at her usual seat. Elsa-May had already plated the food.

"We normally say silent thanks for the food," Florence explained.

"Don't let me stop you," Kelly said.

They closed their eyes to give thanks for the food, and then they started eating.

"Thank you for inviting me. It's rare I get to eat

a meal like this. It's just like my mother used to make when I was a boy."

After some small talk, Ettie figured it might be okay if she slipped in some talk about Dustin.

"How are they doing with Dustin's case?"

"Funny you should mention that. That's why I was late for dinner. Linda Gandara has agreed to give evidence against her husband in exchange for a lighter sentence."

"She knew that he killed those people?" Elsa-May asked.

"Will she have to go to jail?" Ettie asked.

"She lied to us?" Florence asked.

"To answer all your questions, she might have to go to jail, she knew he killed those two people, and she lied to you if she told you otherwise."

"She looked me in the eye and lied to me," Florence said.

After the detective had swallowed another mouthful, he said, "I have a couple of questions for you, Mrs. Lapp. Would you prefer to answer them tomorrow? I could come back here, or you could come into the station."

"I can talk now. As long as Ettie and Elsa-May don't mind."

"We don't at all," Ettie answered for the both of them.

The detective asked Florence, "Who did Morrie marry? Who was his first wife?"

"He didn't marry—he didn't believe in it."

"Well, who was the mother of Morrie's child?" Ettie asked.

"It was Linda Gandara. She eventually married Reginald, Morrie's brother. Didn't I mention that?"

Ettie gasped loudly dropping her fork, which clanged loudly on the table and bounced onto the floor while Elsa-May froze in place.

"Nee! You didn't tell us that, Florence!" Ettie said.

"Why wouldn't you let us know that?" Elsa-May scowled at Florence.

Ettie narrowed her eyes. "I can't believe you didn't tell us that in the first place, Florence! We've been trying to help you all this time and that's something you should've thought to tell us up front."

The detective raised his hand. "There's no need for an argument over this lovely dinner."

"Where was she at the time of Allissa's murder?" Ettie asked Florence

"Who? Linda?" Florence asked.

"Yes."

Elsa-May asked the detective, "You found out that she's Dustin's grandmother?"

"Not until just now." He looked at Florence. "Do you mind answering Ettie's question? Do you know where Linda, Dustin's grandmother, was around the time of Allissa's murder?"

"Why would I know?" Florence said. "She was probably at home."

Kelly jumped up while taking his mobile phone out of his pocket. He stood at the back of the room and made a call.

"I would've thought the police would've followed through with that," Florence whispered to her sisters. "I thought they would know that

Linda was Dustin's grandmother."

"It makes it even more connected now," Ettie said to Elsa-May.

"Jah, it does. They used the gun, then Florence's house gets burned down and the gun's found in Dustin's car."

"Why would Linda put the gun in the car? She loves her grandson." Ettie stared at Florence trying to figure out the missing pieces.

Kelly sat back down. "I've let them know that Linda Gandara is Dustin's grandmother and not just his great aunt by marriage. Dustin's parents are overseas on vacation and no one's been able to reach them."

"Does that change anything?" Florence asked.

Ettie answered, although the question was directed at the detective. "She is Dustin and Darrin's grandmother. Dustin and Darrin were both having problems with Allissa, in one way or another. If Linda looked the other way when her husband killed two people, maybe she wanted this girl out of the way to save her grandson, or grandsons, from being hurt by Allissa."

"That sounds like some fanciful story, Ettie," Florence said.

"People have been killed for less," the detective said.

"Let's just say what Ettie said is correct; how does that explain the gun used in the previous murders being placed in Dustin's car. Also, how did the police know it was there? Because they certainly seemed to know."

Kelly shook his head. "You've made some good points. And because it's not my case, I don't know how to answer you, but I'll look into it. I'll see if I can find out why they stopped his car."

"They said he was swerving over the road, didn't they?" Ettie asked.

"That's what they said, but I'll go to their station where the arrest was made and look in their files."

"They'll let you do that?"

He nodded. "I'm helping them. I got Linda and Reginald Gandara for them. Of course they'll give me access to their files."

"Good!" Ettie was pleased with herself for asking him to dinner. They'd achieved quite a lot.

He looked down at his half-eaten dinner. "I'm sorry to interrupt the dinner. Shall we continue?"

The elderly ladies continued to eat in silence.

When Elsa-May was dishing out apple pie for dessert, Ettie asked, "What about the missing twin? Was he staying at Linda's house?"

He nodded. "It was his laptop, but they still haven't been able to locate him or Reginald. It seems they're both on the run."

"But you said Darrin didn't do anything."

"As far as we're aware he didn't. I shouldn't have said he's on the run. He's missing and wanted for questioning. But they do have a warrant out for Reginald Gandara. So, all's well that ends well," Kelly said.

"No!" Florence said.

"What do you mean?" Ettie asked the detective.

"Well, we still aren't certain how the gun got into Dustin's car, but it didn't have his prints on it and Linda is giving testimony against her husband."

"Dustin didn't kill that girl," Florence insisted.

"The forensic evidence tells us otherwise, Mrs. Lapp."

Ettie didn't comment about knowing about a slap across the face that Allissa had given Dustin. She just hoped that when they found Dustin's brother, he might be able to shed light on everything. After all, he was the one who knew Allissa.

When the detective left, Florence said, "I thought he'd never leave."

"We need to find the twin." Ettie sat on the couch opposite Florence.

"And how are we going to do that?" Elsa-May asked from her favorite chair as she knitted on her latest project.

"Maybe he's hiding out at his grandmother's house?" Ettie suggested.

"Nee, wouldn't the police be watching it?"

Ettie shrugged. "I don't know, but he might be the key to this whole thing."

Chapter 20

The next morning, Ettie called the lawyer to see how everything was lining up.

"Mrs. Smith, I'm glad you called. I've just heard that the police have Reginald and Darrin Gandara."

"They do?"

"Yes."

"That is good news."

"Darrin is being questioned as we speak and Reginald is under arrest. At this stage, Darrin claims to have witnessed his brother arguing with Allissa Thomas on the day she was murdered."

Ettie gasped. That didn't sound good for Dustin. "On campus?"

"Yes."

"Is that good or bad for Dustin?"

"If he tells the police that he saw Dustin get slapped across the face, that'll be good."

"When will you know?"

"I'm not Darrin's lawyer. That would be a

conflict of interests. You might be able to find out if you ask your detective friend. They aren't too forthcoming with me unless they have to tell me something by law."

"I see. I'll visit him this morning. Thank you. I'm glad I called you."

"Let me know as soon as you find out anything."

"I will." Ettie hung up and walked back to the house. Everything now seemed to hinge on Darrin's testimony.

By mid-morning the three sisters were in a taxi heading to the police station.

"I hope Detective Kelly doesn't get sick of seeing us," Florence said.

"He's probably past that already," Elsa-May said.

Ettie nibbled on a fingernail, wondering what excuse she'd give Kelly for coming to the station when they'd only talked to him the night before. She didn't want to let on she'd received information from Dustin's lawyer.

"What are you thinking, Ettie?" Florence asked.

"I'm thinking you should let me do the talking."

When they walked in the door of the station, the officer at the desk pointed to the waiting area as he picked up the phone.

"Will he tell him we're here?" Florence whispered to Ettie.

"*Jah.* He knows us. We always ask to see Kelly."

As soon as they sat down, Kelly walked out and stood in front of them. "Let's go to my office."

He closed the door as soon as they were all inside his office. "You've heard?"

"Heard what?" Ettie asked hoping she wouldn't get caught out.

The detective didn't ask them to sit which Ettie took as a sign he didn't want them to waste his time.

Kelly continued, "We have Darrin right now at the station where you gave your testimony. He witnessed his twin brother killing Allissa Thomas." He looked at Florence. "I'm very sorry, Mrs. Lapp.

I know you wanted this to turn out differently."

"That can't be right. Why did he disappear, then?" Ettie asked.

"He didn't want to testify against his own brother. He was in shock and had to go away and think. When we found him, he agreed to do the right thing and testify."

"I think I asked you this before, but you never found out for me. Did the police get an anonymous tip-off about Dustin?"

"Yes, they did. Someone called them and told them they witnessed Dustin strangling Allissa, and they also saw him with a gun. They gave the police the plate number of the car they saw him get into."

"Did Darrin say he made the call?"

Kelly shook his head. "He made no such call. There must've been another witness to the murder."

"Who called the murder in?" Ettie asked.

"A young lady from the college found her and then called 911."

Elsa-May pulled a face. "That's odd. A man witnesses the murder and calls the police about

Dustin and goes to the trouble to give the police the plate number and doesn't make a call about the woman who was strangled."

Kelly frowned. "I'll look into that. Maybe there was another call to 911, and the young woman made the call first. If you're right, it wouldn't add up."

"Am I right in remembering that Dustin's prints were *not* on the gun?" Ettie asked.

"I believe so, but the gun was in his car. He could've wiped his prints off."

"Isn't it Dustin's word against Darrin's?" Elsa-May asked.

"No, it's not. Dustin isn't saying he saw his brother do it. Dustin is denying knowing the girl, but we know that he knew the girl. We've got dozens of witnesses who confirm that Dustin knew Allissa."

Ettie nodded. Dustin shouldn't have lied about that, now he looked guilty.

"I tried to help you, but sometimes we're wrong about people." Kelly looked down.

Florence pulled out a chair and slumped into it.

"Can I get you anything, Mrs. Lapp?" Kelly asked.

Ettie patted her sister on her shoulder.

"I'm okay. I just need to rest a moment."

"I'll get you a glass of water."

When Kelly stepped out of his office, Elsa-May comforted Florence. Ettie spotted a file on Kelly's desk. She quickly opened it and scanned through the pages.

"We need to talk to Darrin," Ettie hissed. "If we hurry, we can catch him at the other station after they finish questioning him."

Florence swiveled to look at her. "You believe he's innocent? Dustin?"

"Do you?" Ettie asked.

"*Jah,* I know it."

"Then so do I. Have your water, and then tell Kelly you feel much better, but don't look happy, or he'll think we're up to something."

Right then, Kelly walked back in holding a glass of water. He handed the glass to Florence.

She took a couple of sips, while Ettie did her best to look sad.

Florence handed Kelly the glass when she stood up. "Thank you for all you've done."

"It was nothing. Your sisters have been a great help to me over the past years. I was glad to do something to help them."

"Thank you," Ettie said.

The detective's eyes fell to the file on his desk and then focused on Ettie.

"We should get out of your way," Elsa-May said moving closer to the door.

"It's over now, Mrs. Smith. There's nothing more you can do."

Ettie nodded. "I know. Thank you for all you've done."

"Do you mean that?" Kelly asked.

"Come on, Ettie, let's go," Elsa-May said.

"Yes, I thank you." Ettie moved past him out of his office. She wondered why he looked at the file like that. She'd been careful to place it back in the same position that he'd had it.

Chapter 21

Elsa-May hailed a passing taxi as soon as they were on the pavement outside the station. They all sat in the back, and again, Ettie ended up in the middle. This time, she was too involved in the thoughts revolving around in her head to care.

"That was a close call, Ettie," Elsa-May said after she told the driver where they were headed.

"You shouldn't have done that," Florence said.

"What did you find out?"

"Nothing really. But we need to figure this thing out pretty quickly before we talk with Darrin." Ettie nibbled on a fingernail while she thought. If they did nothing, Dustin would end up in prison for life, or worse.

"Ettie, stop chewing on your nails and pull yourself together," Elsa-May ordered.

Ettie pulled her hand away from her mouth.

"Now, we normally go over who could've done it."

"Right!" Ettie agreed. "Now that I know that Darrin made that call against his brother, I'm thinking it was him."

"Where do my gun and my house fire come into it?"

"I don't know. There seems no point to the gun being in his car. Unless the person wanted Dustin to be charged for those murders as well."

"That's a point, Ettie. There were no witnesses to those murders and only the gun could tie the two murders together."

"It's all so mysterious," Florence said.

The taxi driver said, "It sounds like a good mystery. Can you start at the beginning?"

"We would, but our stop is just up here," Elsa-May replied.

They paid the driver and got out of the car as soon as they could.

"What if he's already left?" Florence asked.

"We'll just have to hope he hasn't."

"One of us should go in there and ask if he's still there," Florence suggested.

"Nee, we can't alert them to us being here. They'll want to know who we are. This is a murder investigation," Ettie said.

"Let's sit across there." Elsa-May nodded to a bus-stop bench across the road where they'd get a clear view of the entrance of the station.

"When he comes out. You should ask him questions, Ettie. All three of us shouldn't go," Florence said.

"But if he tells me something I might need one of you as a witness."

"Nee. I think Florence is right, Ettie. Only you should go."

"Okay," Ettie agreed. "But I have no idea what to ask him. If he came out right now, what would I say?"

Ettie's sisters remained silent. None of them could think of a thing.

"Now might be the time to tell us about the charges Morrie's in prison for."

Florence looked straight ahead.

"It was a holdup."

193

"Same as his brother," Elsa-May said.

Florence glared at her older sister.

"Sorry, keep going."

"He made a lot of money, but he spent more than he made. He was at the casino one night and lost a fortune. He pulled out a gun and demanded it back. Of course, he'd been drinking and didn't know what he was doing. His gun went off somehow and killed someone. It wasn't even the dealer. It was someone behind the dealer."

Ettie scratched her neck. Why couldn't her sister have told them that at the start? There was no great secret there.

"The thing was…"

"Florence, is that him?" Elsa-May asked pointing at a young man at the entrance of the station.

"That's him. Quick, Ettie."

Ettie gulped and made her way across the road. What would she say to him? She had hoped all the pieces would've fallen into place by now, but they hadn't.

Darrin was walking down the steps and Ettie

waited at the bottom, off to one side.

"Darrin Gandara?"

He looked her up and down, a little startled. "Yes?"

She opened her mouth, but her heart was pounding so hard that no words were coming out.

"Do I know you?"

His words gave Ettie an idea. "I think you do. You burned down my house."

He laughed and started walking away.

"I have the proof."

He stopped in his tracks and turned to face her. "It was nothing to do with me."

That's when she knew she had him. "Why did you plant the gun in your brother's car?"

"Look lady—what proof are you talking about?"

"Your grandmother told me everything."

His jaw dropped open. "She wouldn't."

"Ah, but she did."

He looked nervously about him. "No, she wouldn't." When Ettie remained silent, he said, "What do you want?"

195

"I want you to tell me why you burned down my house, or I'll give the police my proof."

He frowned at her. "I wasn't the one who burned down your house." He shifted from one foot to the other and shoved his hands in his pockets. "He did it. My brother killed that girl."

"I'm talking about my house."

"What did my grandmother tell you?"

"Enough to go to the police."

"She did it. If she blamed me, she was lying. She told me she could get me a gun, and when she handed it to me, she laughed about burning an Amish woman's house down. I didn't do it, she did."

"Your grandmother burned my house down?"

"That's what she said."

"Why did you want a gun?"

He looked around himself again. "I don't have to answer your questions." He turned on his heel and walked away.

Not content, Ettie followed him. "Why did you want a gun?"

He stopped and turned around. "You wanna know the truth, lady?"

Ettie nodded and hoped she wasn't in danger.

"I was going to shoot Allissa, but my brother did the job for me. I saw my brother strangle her. Then I hid the gun in his car."

"Wiped your prints off, then called the police?"

"What's it to you? I haven't committed a crime."

"You covered up knowledge of arson—that's a crime."

He stepped toward her and Ettie took a step back. His eyes were radiating pure evil and shivers ran down her back. Darrin suddenly looked over Ettie's shoulder, turned and hurried away.

Ettie glanced over her shoulder to see Elsa-May and Florence hurrying toward her. Then Kelly pulled up beside them in his car.

He jumped out of his car. "I thought you all would be here."

Ettie pointed to Darrin. "I talked to him and he said his grandmother burned down Florence's house and gave him the gun."

"He did?"

"Yes, quick get him." Ettie pointed to him and Detective Kelly caught up with him.

"What happened, Ettie? He looked like he was going to hit you."

"He said Linda laughed about burning your house, Florence, and he said she gave him your gun. Then he said he was going to kill Allissa, but then he saw Dustin strangling her, so he hid the gun in Dustin's car."

"And then called the police?" Elsa-May asked.

"That's what he claimed."

Chapter 22

Kelly joined them once more, and Ettie saw Darrin getting into a car down the road.

"What did he say?"

Ettie watched the car drive past them. "Who's driving?" Ettie pointed at the car and Kelly spun around.

"It looks like it could be Andy Watkins. He's got distinctive hair—light and wooly. I remember it distinctly from the picture of him in the file. I'll have to talk to Detective Sanders; he's the lead detective on the case."

"What did Darrin say to you?" Ettie asked.

"He said you accused him of burning your house. He asked if he could sue you for harassment."

"What? He lied!"

"Tell me exactly what he told you, Ettie."

Ettie put her hand on her chest and took a deep breath.

Detective Kelly pointed at her. "This is exactly

the kind of thing I warned you against doing. Lucky for you I guessed you would've been silly enough to come here and try to find Darrin."

"Ettie's shaken," Elsa-May said, "Yelling at her won't help."

"Let's borrow an interview room." Kelly led the way into the police station.

Once they were all seated, Ettie told him everything that Darrin said. "He could've been lying about everything," Ettie said

"Wait here. I'll see what he said while he was here and I'll need to find Sanders. It might take some time, but don't go anywhere!"

"We're fine to wait," Florence said.

"I'll have someone bring you in some hot tea." Kelly left them.

"Florence, you were just about to tell us more about Morrie shooting someone when Ettie had to leave."

"Was I?"

"*Jah.* You said that he accidently shot someone who was standing behind the dealer, and then you said, 'The thing was…' and you never said what the thing was."

Florence sighed. "He shot his manager, the one who was married to Linda."

"But wasn't Linda married to him?"

"He didn't believe in marriage; he had a child with Linda, and Linda went on to marry his manager. Then when he was shot, Linda went on to marry Morrie's brother."

"Didn't look too far, did she," Ettie commented shaking her head.

"I guess it's confusing. It looked like Morrie shot his manager out of jealousy, but he was too drunk to know what he was doing."

"Why didn't you tell us that at the beginning?" Elsa-May asked.

"I thought you wouldn't have believed it was an accident."

Ettie asked Elsa-May, "Could that have anything to do with any of this?"

"Linda had a grudge against Morrie, the father of her son, grandfather of both Dustin and Darrin?"

"You'll have to go and visit Morrie."

"Nee, I couldn't."

"You'll have to."

"Look at me! The last time I saw him, I was young and beautiful. I couldn't let him see me like this. I'm so old now, and wrinkly."

"He'll be old too."

"You don't understand."

The door opened and a young officer brought in three mugs of hot tea.

"I need milk and sugar," Florence said to him.

"Yes, I was going to bring them too. I can't carry everything at once."

"Thank you," Ettie said as the officer left.

Once he'd brought in the milk and sugar, he closed the door behind him.

"How long will your detective be, Ettie? I hate waiting."

"He said it might take some time."

Florence carefully poured in milk and then sugar. "Will you come with me, Ettie?"

"Me?"

She nodded. "Will you?"

Elsa-May nodded from behind Florence, encouraging her to agree. "Okay, I'll go."

"Denke. I'm not looking forward to it. He would've been thinking about me all these years, thinking I look quite different from this."

"We'll make a call and book a visit."

"What if he refuses to see me?"

Ettie leaned forward and placed her hand over Florence's. "At least we would've tried."

"What happened to his music rights?" Ava asked.

"What's that?"

"Well, I believe the music industry has a system whereby the artist gets paid every time their music gets played anywhere."

"How do you know that, Ava?"

"I don't know. I heard about it or read it somewhere."

"Would there be a lot of money involved?"

"Jah quite possibly especially if he was well-known and people still play his music."

"That's something we should ask him, Florence."

Florence shook her head. "No one would remember him. I doubt people listen to his music nowadays. He hasn't been on tour since the fifties."

"Should I look into it?" Ava asked.

"Jah, please do," Ettie said. "We'll call you before our visit."

Chapter 23

Ettie and Florence arrived at the same prison where Dustin was being held.

"Do you think they could've spoken to one another?" Ettie asked.

"Morrie's in maximum security."

"Oh."

They went through the same process as when they'd visited Dustin. Finally, they were seated, waiting for Morrie to appear.

"It's a good sign that they haven't turned us away," Ettie said.

"Do I look all right?" Florence said pinching her cheeks to give them some color.

Ettie squelched a laugh. "You look fine."

Then two guards walked in front of them, behind the barrier, and then a row of prisoners followed. A guard led a man to them and instructed him to sit. He was old, didn't have much hair, but his face was kind. His eyes were fixed onto Florence. Ettie immediately felt sad that this man had spent so many years in prison. In that same time, Florence had married, and had children while the man she once loved was behind bars. A quick glance at Florence and Ettie knew how hard it had been for her sister to walk away and return to the community leaving all thoughts of him behind.

"You've gotten old." Florence giggled.

"You haven't. You're still as beautiful as the last time I saw you."

She smiled.

"You went back to the Amish?"

"I did. I told you that's what I was going to do."

"I'm glad you went back and carried on without me. Did you marry?"

Florence nodded and Ettie saw tears form in her eyes.

"I'm Florence's sister." Ettie thought it a good time to speak up since Florence seemed to forget she was there.

"This is my sister, Ettie."

"Hello." He nodded and then looked back at

Florence. "Why are you here after all this time?"

"Have you heard about your grandsons?"

"What about them?"

"Has either of them been to see you lately?" Ettie asked.

He scratched his cheek. "They've both visited me from time to time, but not lately. Why?"

"Morrie, who owns your music rights now?"

"Is this about those papers I signed?"

"What papers?" Florence asked.

"Darrin wanted me to sign the rights over so he could do something with my music. The industry's changed so much. They don't have records anymore. Now they've got CDs and downloads."

"You gave your rights to Darrin?" Ettie asked.

He looked at Ettie. "No. I gave them to Darrin and Dustin. I made certain that both names were on the contract." He shrugged his shoulders. "Someone might as well be making money out of my music. It's no good to me in here."

"Will you ever get out?" Florence asked.

"Florrie, I don't think so."

Now Ettie knew why Florence had bristled when Detective Kelly called her Florrie. She only wanted to be called Florrie by the man she once loved. Ettie tried to stop a smile that was tugging at the corners of her lips when she thought of the names they'd called one another—Morrie and Florrie.

"Did you hear that Reginald's in trouble?"

"I heard it on the news. We've got television in here. I heard he was arrested for two murders. How did you know?"

"Reginald and Linda have kept in touch over the years. I met one of your grandsons too."

"Which one, Dustin?"

"Yes, how did you know?"

"Darrin isn't too sociable. I thought it would've been Dustin. He writes to me."

"Time's up."

They looked up to see a large corrections officer standing over Morrie.

Morrie leaned forward. "I'll have to go. You don't need to come back. I'm okay."

"Can I write?"

He nodded. "Okay, but I'm never getting out of here. I want you to know that."

"Let's go," the officer said.

Morrie stood up and was escorted away.

Ettie saw that Florence was blinking back tears. "Let's go," Ettie echoed the officer.

On the way back home in the taxi, Ettie said, "So, both grandsons have the rights to his music."

Florence whispered, "If Dustin was convicted of murder would that mean Darrin would get everything?"

Ettie thought about it for a while. "It would certainly make it easy for Darrin to somehow get his hands on the lot."

"We need to tell his lawyer."

"We will, but first I think we need to get you home."

"*Jah,* it's taken quite a bit out of me. I'd be grateful for a rest."

When they got home, the first thing Ettie did was tell Elsa-May what they found out.

"Can I lie down on your bed, Ettie?" Florence asked.

"Of course."

When Florence was out of the room, Elsa-May said, "Darrin had a motive to get Dustin out of the way—in jail. It appears he's framed him, but what about Allissa?"

Chapter 24

Kelly arrived at their house looking smug. "I've got a lot to tell you."

"Come inside and sit down."

"We've arrested Darrin. He admitted to framing his twin and burning down your house, Mrs. Lapp and placing the gun in Dustin's car and also admitted to making that anonymous call to the police to implicate his twin."

"Did he kill Allissa?" Ettie asked.

"He says not. That's how we were able to get him to admit to everything else. You see, through a stroke of good fortune, we found that he got a speeding ticket close to your house, Mrs. Lapp, on the morning your house burned down. He couldn't give us a good reason for being in that area, and then when we tried to tie him to Allissa's murder, he sang like a canary."

"What?" Elsa-May asked.

"He witnessed Allissa's murder because he was

following her. He saw his brother have an argument with her and saw Allissa slap Dustin's face—just as Dustin eventually admitted to us. Then when she was heading to her car, Darrin saw that Watkins confronted her and then those two argued. He watched Andy Watkins strangle Allissa."

"Why didn't he stop him?"

"He could've been afraid. Watkins isn't a small man. He stands at six feet four and is nearly as wide. Darrin hates his brother. He claims to have already hidden the gun in Dustin's car earlier that day; then he made the call to the police."

Ettie nibbled on a fingernail. "Do you believe him?"

"It makes sense."

"Does it? Why were they in the same car? You saw them."

"I thought it was Andy Watkins, going by his photo, but I couldn't see in the car too well."

"What was his purpose for getting my gun in the first place?" Florence asked.

Ettie said, "Maybe his great-uncle Reginald

bragged about killing two people and told him where the gun was. He put the gun in Dustin's car and was going to call the police to have him arrested for those two holdup murders. Then when he saw Allissa murdered, he thought quickly. Why not have his brother arrested for Allissa's murder as well?"

"I don't think so, Ettie," Florence said. "If he loved this woman, Allissa, how could he be so quick-thinking after watching her murder?"

"Ah, the criminal mind works differently from your mind and my mind, Mrs. Lapp. They are on a different playing field—a different level of thought. They do wrong, because they can do wrong—they enjoy it," Kelly said.

"Did you arrest Andy Watkins?" Elsa-May asked.

"He's being questioned. We've already got someone arrested for her murder."

"So you've arrested Darrin for burning down my house?"

"Yes, and there will likely be more charges

heading his way."

"Does that mean that Dustin will go free?" Florence asked.

"Things will be sorted out in due course. He's still in custody at present."

He looked over at Florence. "On a different note, I made some inquiries and found out that your friend has a hearing tomorrow. He might get out, if all goes well. He's served his time."

"A hearing?"

"Yes."

"He never mentioned that."

"You're still in touch with him?"

Ettie kicked Florence's foot, hoping she'd keep quiet about their visit to the prison to see Morrie.

"Something wrong, Ettie?"

"Nee, just that my foot was going to sleep."

He frowned at Ettie and looked back at Florence. "You keep in touch with him?"

"Yes."

Elsa-May said, "Detective, how about a cup of coffee?"

"No, thank you. That'll only keep me awake. I'll be on my way. I thought you ladies would appreciate an update on things." He stood up. "I'll look into those points you raised, Ettie."

Ettie stood up and walked him to the door. When she closed the door, she turned around to face Florence who was right behind her.

"Ettie, he's getting out."

"I heard."

"It's a hearing, he might not get out."

Florence turned around to look at her older sister. "Elsa-May, you must believe he'll get out."

"Why must I?"

After sitting back down, she said, "Because he's been in there long enough. He didn't do it deliberately."

"I think we all need a cup of hot tea," Ettie said.

Florence followed Ettie and Elsa-May into the kitchen. "I know what you're thinking. That we shouldn't mix with the outside world. He's an *Englischer* and not likely ever to join us."

"It has to be your choice if you see him when he

gets out," Ettie said as she filled the pot with water.

"What do you think, Elsa-May?"

"It's a hard decision but you've stayed on the narrow road for all these years, it would be a shame to fall off the road when you're so close to your journey's end."

"*Denke* for cheering me up. So I'll soon be dead."

Elsa-May chuckled. "We're all not long for this earth. All of us, our bodies will wear out sooner or later, and you'd want to be ready."

Florence nodded.

Ettie joined them at the table. "You could visit him but don't bring him into your life. I know you loved him once, but if you'd stayed with him things might not have been so rosy."

"I have thought about that. It might be the idea of love, and remembering what we had. I might be remembering it better than it actually was."

"That's right," Elsa-May said.

"I'm glad you've both been with me through my hard times. It's not easy having no home, having to be a burden on others."

"We've loved having you here," Ettie said.

"You both make me see sense."

Elsa-May changed the subject. "What do you think of the way everything turned out?"

Ettie breathed out heavily. "It's not over yet."

"It won't be over until they release Dustin," Florence said. "I knew he wasn't guilty. I said that right from the start."

"Jah, you did." Ettie pushed herself up from the table to take the pot off the stove.

Chapter 25

The next day, Ettie answered a knock on the door.

Ava stood in front of her.

"Ava, come in."

Ava walked inside and the three elderly sisters told her what Detective Kelly had told them the night before.

"Well, that's why I'm here. After I was helping my *mudder* at the markets, I stopped to have a cup of coffee and they had a television on the wall. I heard that Andy Watkins was arrested for Allissa's murder."

"What else did they say?" Ettie asked.

"That's all I heard."

"So, if they have arrested him, that means Dustin should be freed," Florence said.

Ava shrugged. "I guess so. That would make sense."

They'd only just sat down when there was

another knock on their door. Ettie opened it to see Detective Kelly standing there with Dustin next to him.

"He wanted to come here to thank you. Is Florence here?" Kelly asked.

Ettie stepped aside. "Come in."

Florence hurried toward him. "You're free?"

"Yes." He laughed and ran a hand through his hair. "I need to go home and get cleaned up, but I just wanted to thank you for everything you've done."

"Ettie and Elsa-May helped too."

"And Ava," Ettie added.

He nodded. "I know. I thank you all, and you too, Detective Kelly." He glanced at Kelly and then turned to the elderly sisters. "If it weren't for all of you I might have spent the rest of my life in jail."

Kelly gave him a pat on his back.

"Can we get you anything?" Elsa-May asked.

He shook his head. "All I want is a proper bed and a hot shower. The shower first."

"I'll drive you home," Kelly said.

"Thank you." Dustin looked at Florence. "I had nothing to do with your house burning down."

"I never thought for one moment that you did anything wrong."

"Darrin's admitted to that," said Kelly, "and a few other things, as I told you yesterday."

"I'm just glad that the truth has come out," Dustin said.

He smiled before he walked out with Kelly.

Ettie looked at Florence to see her face beaming. "I'm so happy how things ended."

"Me too," Elsa-May said.

The three sisters along with Ava watched out the living room window as Dustin walked with Kelly to the car.

"That was very nice of your detective to help us in the way that he did. He didn't have to."

"Eh! I suppose he's all right," Ettie said.

"He's getting better," Elsa-May added.

Ava laughed. "What's happening is that the two of you are wearing him down."

After that....

Two weeks later, Florence and Dustin were waiting for Morrie when he was released from prison.

Florence wanted to be there when he got out.

He found an apartment close to Dustin, and Morrie did his best to adapt to life on the outside.

Keeping to her faith, Florence kept her distance even though Morrie shared with her the news that he'd accepted the Lord as his Savior while he'd been in prison. They organized a regular meeting place where they had coffee together once a week.

"We're going to get married," Florence announced to her sisters six months later.

"What?" Ettie asked staring at her in disbelief.

"Can I come inside?" Florence asked.

"Of course you can."

Elsa-May hurried toward Florence, leaving her knitting on the chair she'd just been sitting on. "You're marrying Morrie?"

"I am."

Ettie was pleased for her sister and pleased for Morrie. Knowing from her sister's letters that Morrie had been to the last few of her Sunday meetings, she guessed that Morrie was joining the community.

"He's talked to the bishop?" Elsa-May inquired.

"Jah, he has."

Ettie asked, "Won't he miss the outside world?"

"Nee, he says it's too fast for him. He doesn't like the pace of things. Don't you see? Things have worked out. I've missed him so much and never dared to even think something like this would happen."

Elsa-May tilted her head to one side. "So, he believes in marriage now?"

Florence giggled like a girl. "He does."

"Sit down and tell us everything," Elsa-May pulled her sister over to the couch.

Once Florence was seated, Elsa-May picked up her knitting and sat back down on her chair.

Ettie sat down beside Florence and enjoyed

listening to a most unusual love story. She already knew the facts from all of Florence's recent letters, but it was more exciting to listen to them in person and watch the excitement on her sister's face.

Fear thou not; for I am with thee: be not dismayed;
for I am thy God: I will strengthen thee; yea,
I will help thee; yea,
I will uphold thee with the right hand of my
righteousness.
Isaiah 41:10

Thank you for your interest in
'Amish False Witness'
Ettie Smith Amish Mysteries Book 8

* * * * * * * * * * * * * *

For Samantha Price's New Release alerts join
Samantha email list at:
www.samanthapriceauthor.com

Other books in this series:
Ettie Smith Amish Mysteries Book 1

Secrets Come Home

After Ettie Smith's friend, Agatha, dies, Ettie is surprised to find that Agatha has left her a house. During building repairs, the body of an Amish man who disappeared forty years earlier is discovered under the floorboards.

When it comes to light that Agatha and the deceased man were once engaged to marry, the police declare Agatha as the murderer.

Ettie sets out to prove otherwise.

Soon Ettie hears rumors of stolen diamonds, rival criminal gangs, and a supposed witness to the true murderer's confession.

When Ettie discovers a key, she is certain it holds the answers she is looking for.

Will the detective listen to Ettie's theories when he sees that the key belongs to a safe deposit box?

Ettie Smith Amish Mysteries Book 2
<u>Amish Murder</u>

When a former Amish woman, Camille Esh, is murdered, the new detective in town is frustrated that no one in the Amish community will speak to him. The detective reluctantly turns to Ettie Smith for help. Soon after Ettie agrees to see what she can find out, the dead woman's brother, Jacob, is arrested for the murder. To prove Jacob's innocence, Ettie delves into the mysterious and secretive life of Camille Esh, and uncovers one secret after another.

Will Ettie be able to find proof that Jacob is innocent, even though the police have DNA evidence against him, and documentation that proves he's guilty?

Can Ettie uncover the real murderer amongst the many people who had reasons to want Camille dead?

Ettie Smith Amish Mysteries Book 3:
<u>Murder in the Amish Bakery</u>

When Ettie has problems with her bread sinking in the middle, she turns to her friend, Ruth Fuller, who owns the largest Bakery in town.

When Ruth and Ettie discover a dead man in Ruth's Bakery with a knife in his back, Ruth is convinced the man was out to steal her bread recipe.

It was known that the victim, Alan Avery, was one of the three men who were desperate to get their hands on Ruth's bread secrets.

When it's revealed that Avery owed money all over town, the local detective believes he was after the large amount of cash that Ruth banks weekly.

Why was Alan Avery found with a Bible clutched in his hand? And what did it have to do with a man who was pushed down a ravine twenty years earlier?

Ettie Smith Amish Mysteries Book 4

Amish Murder Too Close

Elderly Amish woman, Ettie Smith, finds a body outside her house. Everything Ettie thought she knew about the victim is turned upside down when she learns the dead woman was living a secret life. As the dead woman had been wearing an engagement ring worth close to a million dollars, the police must figure out whether this was a robbery gone wrong. When an Amish man falls under suspicion, Ettie has no choice but to find the real killer.

What information about the victim is Detective Kelly keeping from Ettie?

When every suspect appears to have a solid alibi, will Ettie be able to find out who murdered the woman, or will the Amish man be charged over the murder?

Book 5
Amish Quilt Shop Mystery

Amish woman, Bethany Parker, finally realizes her dream of opening her own quilt shop. Yet only days after the grand opening, when she invites Ettie Smith to see her store, they discover the body of a murdered man.

At first Bethany is concerned that the man is strangely familiar to her, but soon she has more pressing worries when she discovers her life is in danger.

Bethany had always been able to rely on her friend, Jabez, but what are his true intentions toward her?

Book 6
Amish Baby Mystery

Ettie and her sister, Elsa-May, find an abandoned baby boy wrapped in an Amish quilt on their doorstep. Ettie searches for clues as to the baby's identity and finds a letter in the folds of the quilt. The letter warns that if they don't keep the baby hidden, his life will be in danger.

When the retired Detective Crowley stumbles onto their secret, they know they need to find the baby's mother fast.

Will Ettie and Elsa-May be able to keep the baby safe and reunite him with his parents before it's too late?

What does the baby have to do with a cold case kidnapping that happened years before?

Book 7

Betrayed

When Amish woman, Paula Peters, is brutally attacked and left for dead, Detective Kelly requests that elderly Ettie Smith and her sister, Elsa-May, ask questions within their Amish community. The detective arrests a local woman for the attack, but Ettie and Elsa-May suspect that she has been framed. When they discover that the woman's husband, Cameron George, is Paula's former boss, they are more than certain they're right. The problem is, Cameron is a former police officer, and Detective Kelly insists that Ettie is wrong about him. When Detective Kelly finally concedes that the woman might have been framed, he turns his suspicions to a young Amish man. Can Ettie and Elsa-May find evidence that Cameron has framed his wife before Kelly arrests another innocent person for the crime? Will Paula wake up and identify the person responsible for assaulting her?

Samantha Price loves to hear from her readers.
Connect with Samantha at:
samanthaprice333@gmail.com
http://www..com/AmishRomance
http://www.samanthapriceauthor.com
http://www.facebook.com/SamanthaPriceAuthor